中国经典古诗词100首英译研究

张琼 著

Lakeside Poetic Breeze

English Translation of

100 Classic Chinese Poems

图书在版编目(CIP)数据

湖畔诗风:中国经典古诗词100首英译研究＝Lakeside Poetic Breeze:English Translation of 100 Classic Chinese Poems/张琼著.—武汉:武汉大学出版社,2020.9(2022.4重印)

ISBN 978-7-307-21651-8

Ⅰ.湖… Ⅱ.张… Ⅲ.古典诗歌—英语—文学翻译—研究—中国 Ⅳ.①I207.22 ②H315.9

中国版本图书馆 CIP 数据核字(2020)第 129379 号

责任编辑:李晶晶　　责任校对:汪欣怡　　版式设计:韩闻锦

出版发行:**武汉大学出版社**　(430072　武昌　珞珈山)
(电子邮箱:cbs22@whu.edu.cn　网址:www.wdp.com.cn)
印刷:武汉邮科印务有限公司
开本:720×1000　1/16　印张:15　字数:193 千字　插页:1
版次:2020 年 9 月第 1 版　2022 年 4 月第 2 次印刷
ISBN 978-7-307-21651-8　定价:45.00 元

版权所有,不得翻印;凡购我社的图书,如有质量问题,请与当地图书销售部门联系调换。

爱诗，译诗，论诗
——张琼译诗"三部曲"序

吴伟雄

张琼君的译诗"三部曲"包括：《湖畔诗风——中国经典古诗词100首英译研究》（武汉大学出版社）、《湖畔诗意——中国当代诗歌100首英译研究》（芝加哥学术出版社）、《湖畔诗桥——100首诗歌中英互译研究》（武汉大学出版社）。这"三部曲"从古至今，从中到外，总结了她多年来爱诗、译诗和论诗的丰硕成果。可喜可贺！她嘱我为之写序。我虽然也说得上爱诗、译过诗和写过一些论诗的文字，但水平有限，成果甚微，仍是一名票友，所以曾数次婉拒。但感于张君一再有嘱，且近年来一直和她就诗学问题展开讨论交流，还和她共同在武汉大学出版社出版《中英诗歌鉴赏》，诚意实在难违，只好奉命为之。

与诗结缘三步走：爱诗，译诗，论诗。

张君是肇庆学院外国语学院副教授，翻译研究所副所长，翻译学科带头人；广东省肇庆市翻译协会会长，华诗会会员及汉英双语诗刊《诗殿堂》翻译部执行主编。

在大学阶段，她就喜欢诗歌，买过诗集赏读，在大学执教翻译时，曾到中山大学进修，买了诗歌著作学习和研读。爱诗、赏读、研读之余，其五年前曾就唐代诗人王维《鹿柴》一诗的英译写了两篇研究论文——《〈鹿柴〉六个英译本的语篇功能分析》和《〈鹿柴〉六个英译本的经验功能分析》——在高校学报发表。可见她的研读,并非浮光掠影,而是渐入深度。她说,真正"恋上诗歌"是2018年夏天从《译原》电子杂志和中诗网"英诗同题翻译"栏目上译诗开始的。

自两年前爱上诗歌起,她就真正走上了译诗之路。《译原》电子杂志大概每月征译两期,古体诗和现代诗交替进行;《英诗同题翻译》大概每月一期。从一发端,她就一发不可收拾,尽管工作很忙,仍几乎不缺席上述两个平台每期的译文征集活动!

其译诗,走的是"译旧似旧""译新似新"的路子,最大的特色是以诗译诗,行文简洁,而无诗行膨胀的感觉;另外,其所译诗歌意思清晰,语义连贯,意境明朗,语法脉络和逻辑思路清楚。在用韵方面,其逐渐掌握了规律,韵式也逐步运用自如。

她完成征集译文后,还在译文之后,写上"译后小记"(或"译论""译评"),总结思路和技巧。其每期征译用热情做,"用力"实践,在量的方面积累经验;译后则"用心"总结,在质的方面提高,如怎样翻译(how),为什么这样翻译(why)。英语谚语有云:The person who knows how will always have a job. But the person who knows why will be boss(知其然者,任事;知其所以然者,任人)。且把"任人"理解为翻译的主人,掌握翻译的主动权吧。果然,近两年,她又在国内外刊物上陆续发表了四篇诗歌翻译研究论文,如《诗歌翻译,连贯重构与诗意再现——以司各特的〈狩猎歌〉为例》。

她对诗歌翻译是研究,已经不囿于"译"了,而且还涉足歌曲译配。所谓"译配",就是不仅仅单纯翻译诗歌一样的歌词,还必须让译出的歌词戴着原曲旋律的"镣铐",配合得当,自然顺畅地唱出来、唱得好!她译配的作品,陆续在中诗网和海外的"英国文学"电子平台发表,备受好评。她还撰写研究歌曲译配的学术论文。此外,她还在《诗殿堂》等诗刊发表自己的原创诗作。

张君译诗"三部曲",是她与诗结缘——爱诗,译诗,论诗——三步走的结果,对有意与诗结缘的朋友有一定的启发和帮助。这大概可以形象地喻为——

学诗者的入门小苑。

初学诗的年轻人,可能觉得诗歌很难。我曾在大学开设"英语诗歌选读"课,有的学生心生疑问,"诗歌是不是很难呀?"其实,写诗,译诗,当然很难;但是,选读英语诗歌,而不是写和译啊!初学,可以选短小的诗歌学习。张君的译诗"三部曲"涉及古今中外的300首诗词,如果将其比作琳琅满目的自助餐,可以一道道地品尝,又可以根据喜好选尝,开卷一读,积少成多,终有收益。现在一些住宅,一进门就是"入户花园",这"三部曲",就起到学诗者的入门小苑的作用了。

译诗者的交流平台。

诗无达诂,译无定译。译者如何理解,译文就如何写成。以宋代诗人陈与义诗《拒霜》的英译为例,可作说明。诗曰:

> 拒霜花已吐,吾宇不凄凉。天地虽肃杀,草木有芬芳。道人宴坐处,侍女古时妆。浓露湿丹脸,西风吹绿裳。

张君在"译后小记"上写道:"诗题'拒霜'的英译是个难点,若单纯音译不能表达其义;若按字面直译为 the frost-proof blooms,则不知为何种花卉;若用其学名似难出诗意诗境。笔者曾采用音译+意译,译为 Jushuang, the Frost-Proof Blooms。简洁一点,以 cotton rose(木芙蓉)也未尝不可,诗文中写的就是拒霜不畏严寒,只是丢失"拒霜"这一中文花名,加大了读者的理解难度。诗无达诂,翻译总是得失之间的选择。"

这一期所有应征译文发表后,她把全部译文进行了研究梳理,不仅分析各译家对诗题的不同翻译，还分析了个人对"天地""草木"的不同理解，"道人""侍女"的意象差异，"侍女"与"拒霜"的关系，等等。

读者在选读其"三部曲"个别诗及其译文的时候，可以根据自己的理解，得出不同的结果（译文），实际上是和译者进行译诗的交流。

论诗者的思路发端。

张君译诗"三部曲"后面的"译后小记"是一大独特特点。这是译者理解思路，技巧说明，或译诗理论的小结。"译后小记"是写诗歌翻译研究论文的发端。西南大学文旭教授说，翻译及翻译学研究最好的办法就是把规定、描写、解释融为一体，把 what, why, how 这三个问题结合起来，张君的诗歌翻译研究正是走的这一路线。所以，她近两年能在海内外期刊连续发表四篇诗歌翻译研究论文。

对此，本人亦颇有体会和实践。笔者有一位从事医疗工作的高中学友申报副高级职称时，写了论文《手术治疗子宫脱垂的体会》，请我把论文摘要译为英语。我的译文，得到其校（现广州医科大学）教授的赞许，说"译得比学校年轻的英语教师好"。我就思考，"好在什么地方呢?"我总结出：除去枝叶，抓住主干；通盘考虑，信达求雅；不必形似，但求神似；专有名词，名从主人。这是我第一次写的"译后小记"，后来扩展成文——《理解理顺原文，译文才有条理——英译一篇妇产科医学论文摘要的体会》。此文在《中国科技翻译》1995 年第 3 期发表（知网可查）。后来，这位学友申报正高级职称写的论文，也让我英译其论文摘要。笔者还曾应中国海洋大学硕士生导师兼外事处首席翻译邹卫宁之约，为该校英译校训"海纳百川，取则行远"。邹老师客气地回函说："I think your translation of the 'mission statement' of our university is quite 'faithful, expressive and elegant'." 就译文是怎样组织出来的这个问题，我写了"英译小记"，全文在《中国海洋大学报》上发表，还附上我的简介。

"译后小记",作用不小!

以诗译诗,脱离不了押韵问题。张君从不大注意韵译到认真实践韵译,爱上韵译,最后"译旧似旧",好,实在是好(It's not just good, but wonderful)!韵译产生"音美"。然而,"意美"是硬道理!韵译诗歌,必须警惕"以韵害意"。我愿和张君以及坚持"译旧似旧"的同好们共勉!诗歌是视觉的艺术,也是听觉的艺术,是时间的艺术,也是空间的艺术。写诗,译诗,诗歌翻译与研究需要时间的沉淀,不断地进取,希望张君坚持对诗歌及诗歌翻译的酷爱,加强诗学研究,在诗歌翻译与研究上继续新的探索。

我诚意地向诗歌翻译爱好者推荐张君的译诗"三部曲"。先睹为快(The sooner to read, the happier in deed)!

(吴伟雄,中国翻译协会第四、五届理事、资深翻译家;长期从事地方外事单位管理和翻译工作,2006—2017年任北京理工大学珠海学院外国语学院教授。)

前　言

当詹姆斯·鲍斯韦尔问塞缪尔·约翰逊"什么是诗歌?"约翰逊这样回答:"先生,说什么不是诗歌要容易得多。我们都知道什么是光,但不容易说清楚光是什么。"为了便于理解,我们不妨再看看下面这两首诗,以及笔者拙译。

1. What Is Poetry?
By Eleanor Farjeon

What is Poetry? Who knows?
Not a rose, but the scent of the rose;
Not the sky, but the light in the sky;
Not the fly, but the gleam of the fly;
Not the sea, but the sound of the sea;
Not myself, but what makes me
See, hear, and feel something that prose
Cannot: and what it is, who knows?

1. 何为诗
埃莉诺·法杰恩

何为诗,孰知之乎?

非玫瑰，乃其香也，
非天空，乃其光也，
非萤虫，乃其亮也，
非大海，乃其声也。
非吾身，乃触吾心，
感吾耳目，而散文之不能也，
何为诗，孰知之乎？

2. Ars Poetica

By Archibald Macleish

A poem should be palpable and mute
As a globed fruit,

Dumb
As old medallions to the thumb,

Silent as the sleeve-worn stone
Of casement ledges where the moss has grown—

A poem should be wordless
As the flight of birds.

*

A poem should be motionless in time
As the moon climbs,

Leaving, as the moon releases
Twig by twig the night-entangled trees,

Leaving, as the moon behind the winter leaves,

Memory by memory the mind—

A poem should be motionless in time

As the moon climbs.

*

A poem should be equal to:

Not true.

For all the history of grief

An empty doorway and a maple leaf.

For love

The leaning grasses and two lights above the sea—

A poem should not mean

But be.

2. 诗艺
阿奇博尔德·麦克利什

诗应静默而可感知

如滚圆果子

不语

如旧奖章之于拇指

不言如衣袖磨平
的窗台石，青苔悄生——

无声
如鸟翱翔
　　　　　＊
诗应静驻时光
任月攀升

隽永，任月一枝一枝
解开被黑夜纠缠的树

隽永，任月在冬身后离去
记忆于心田——

诗应静驻时光
任月攀升
　　　　　＊
诗不应
写实

人生寂寥
化作空阶枫叶飘

爱意缠绵
化作芳草依依光数点——

诗不言
而是也

    笔者喜爱诗歌，偶尔兴起，也会写几行，真正译诗却还有个缘起。戊戌年仲夏，吴伟雄教授给我发来一首诗，我们探讨了一下翻译。过两日，问我还要修改吗，这才得知，吴教授在《译原》电子杂志翻译诗歌，邀我参与。就这样，从事多年翻译教学的我开始尝试诗歌翻译。翁显良教授曾说：外国文学作品的汉译，其成败关键，在于得作者之志，用汉语之长，求近似的效果。如何才能得作者之志呢，我有幸跟随王东风教授学习语篇翻译，语篇的连贯分析、情景再现有助于理解原诗。遇到诗歌的格律韵式不懂，我就请教吴教授或求助于书本。随着时间的推移，我的译诗也散见于中诗网和《译原》《翻译中国》《暮雪诗刊》《长江诗歌》《中国诗影响》《诗殿堂》《肇庆学院学报》等报纸杂志。于是，我整理了自己翻译的部分诗歌，并撰写译论，集结成这个小册子，以求教于方家。

    鲁迅先生曾提出关于中国文学创作的"三美"理论："意美以感心，一也；音美以感耳，二也；形美以感目，三也。"翻译家许渊冲先生，就将鲁迅的"三美"论进行移植诗歌翻译，从而形成基于其本身翻译诗歌实践的"三美"论。在许渊冲先生看来，在翻译诗歌过程中，追求"真"和"美"并不冲突，追求美在一定程度上也保存了原诗的真，诗歌追求美，翻译追求真。诗无达诂，译无定法。诗歌翻译是有遗憾的艺术，正如屠岸先生所说，不论译者怎样忠实于原作，译作和原作之间总会存在距离，百分之百原汁原味的诗歌翻译是不存在的。据说美国诗人弗罗斯特曾说，Poetry is what gets lost in translation（诗意乃翻译中失去的东西），意味着诗歌翻译难以完美。

    诗歌翻译，笔者尽量以格律诗译格律诗，以自由诗译自由诗，诗歌的音韵节奏，有时甚至标点符号，尽量与原诗一致，尽力传递所译诗歌的原貌。我追求译诗意义不背原诗,语义清晰,行文流畅,有画面感,自然去雕饰,尽量少用注。诗歌翻译我们一直在路上,尽力在"求真""求美"之间找一个最佳平衡点。以下略述二三例。

以诗译诗,译旧如旧。《春日》是宋代思想家、教育家朱熹创作的一首诗。此诗表面上看似一首写景诗,描绘了春日美好的景致;实际上是一首哲理诗,表达了诗人于乱世中追求圣人之道的美好愿望。全诗寓理趣于形象之中,构思运笔堪称奇妙。在翻译这首诗时,我们采用五音步抑扬格为主旋律,押韵格式为aabb。原诗与译诗如下。

3. 春日

〔宋〕朱熹

胜日寻芳泗水滨,
无边光景一时新。
等闲识得东风面,
万紫千红总是春。

3. Spring Day

By Zhu Xi

I'm seeking scenes by Si River on a sunny day;
Grass lush, flowers blooming, a thriving way.
Refreshed by a sudden breath of spring in air,
I see in myriads of colors spring hide there.

译新如新,保留原诗的意象,行文流畅。如海子的《九月》,这首诗歌极其沉痛,充满神秘氛围,渺远的时间与旷阔的空间扭结纠缠在一起,生命与死亡在互相诠释,翻译就是体验和再现诗人所感所想。

诗人借助"草原""野花""秋风""马头琴""明月"等意象，营造旷远深邃的悲秋寂寥，故将"九月"译为 Lunar September，因为农历的九月有更多的文化遐想。翻译时坚持"译意不译字"，如"我的琴声呜咽"，译为 My strings sob(我的琴在呜咽)；"泪水全无"，不译 without tears，而译为 with tearless grief(欲哭无泪的悲伤)。原诗和拙译如下。

4. 九月

海子

目击众神死亡的草原上野花一片
远在远方的风比远方更远
我的琴声呜咽 泪水全无
我把这远方的远归还草原
一个叫马头 一个叫马尾
我的琴声呜咽 泪水全无

远方只有在死亡中凝聚野花一片
明月如镜高悬草原映照千年岁月
我的琴声呜咽 泪水全无
只身打马过草原

4. Lunar September

By Haizi

The prairie witnessed the death of pantheon presents boundless wild flowers
The wind afar is even farther away from afar
My strings sob with tearless grief

I return to the prairie the afar from afar

One is called horse-head, the other horse-tail

My strings sob with tearless grief

The afar only in death converges a sheet of wild flowers

The mirror-like moon hangs high over the land reflecting time of thousands of years

My strings sob with tearless grief

Alone I ride a horse across the prairie

　　诗歌节奏如同呼吸，非常重要，下面举一例说明再现原诗节奏。美国诗人艾米莉·狄金森的诗歌主要写生活情趣、自然、生命等，诗风凝练、比喻新颖、喜用格律、不顾语法，极富独创性。她的 *A Bird Came down the Walk* 是一首白描诗，诗人偶遇一只小鸟吃虫，主角是小鸟，"我"是旁观者。狄金森用简洁的笔触勾勒出小鸟的形象，用小鸟怡然自得捕食蚯蚓、饮水、让路等一连串的动作(came down, bit, ate, drank, hopped, glanced, stirred, unrolled, rowed)去塑造自己，而作者却隐蔽起来(I saw, I thought)，后来因"我"的介入(I offered)，惊扰了小鸟的安宁，结果小鸟展翅飞走。全诗共分 5 个诗节，每节 4 行，只有一个句号，是一个完整连贯的动画。原诗以抑扬格三音步为主旋律(只有每节第三行是四音步)，拙译保留原诗格律和节奏，保留原诗标点符号，以顿代步，尽量再现原文的音韵节奏。

5. A Bird Came Down the Walk
By Emily Dickinson

A Bird /came down /the Walk—

He did/ not know /I saw—

He bit/ an Ang/le Worm/ in halves

And ate /the fel/low, raw,

And then/ he drank /a Dew

From a /conve/nient Grass—

And then/ hopped side/wise to /the Wall

To let/ a Bee/tle pass—

He glanced /with rap/id eyes

That hur/ried all /around—

They looked /like fright/ened Beads, /I thought—

He stirred/ his Vel/vet Head

Like one/ in danger, / Cautious,

I of/fered him/ a Crumb

And he/ unro/lled his /feathers

And rowed/ him sof/ter home—

Than Oars /divide /the Ocean,

Too sil/ver for /a seam—

Or But/terflies, /off Banks /of Noon

Leap, / plashless /as they swim.

5. 小鸟沿小径走来

[美]艾米莉·狄金森

小鸟/沿小径/走来——

不知/一旁/我在瞧——

他把/一条/蚯蚓/啄开
再吃掉/那家伙，/生嚼，

他将/清露/饮吞
取自/近旁/草叶上——
又侧身/跳到/旁边/墙脚根
来给/甲虫/把路让——

急促地/左顾/右盼
他那/滴溜溜的/眼眸——
活像/受惊的/珠子，/我想——
见他/抖了抖/天鹅绒的头

好像/身处险境，/十分小心，
我给他/分点/碎面包
而他/立刻/展开/羽翎
往回/飞去/一路轻飘——

胜过/船桨/划海面，
波光/银白/水无痕——
胜过/蝴蝶，/晌午/草埂边
跃下，/游弋/无溅声。

《湖畔诗风——中国经典古诗词100首英译研究》《湖畔诗意——中国现代诗歌100首英译研究》《湖畔诗桥——100首诗歌中英互译研究》是一个诗歌翻译系列，古代诗歌追求诗风，现代诗追求诗意，中英诗歌互译谓之诗桥。本书《湖畔诗风——中国经典古诗词100首英译研究》选取从先秦时期到清朝的 100 首中国经典古诗词，按朝代顺序编排，部分翻译诗歌在相关电子刊物和纸媒已经发表，编入本书时有所修正，并增加"译后小记"。本书适合于大学英语专业和非英语专业学生、英语教师、诗歌爱好者和诗歌翻译人员阅读、参考。欢迎方家批评指正！

诗歌和诗歌的翻译，提高了我的感性素质和审美情趣，加深了我对生活的体验和认知，让我精神愉悦。译路走来，首先得感谢北京理工大学珠海学院外国语学院吴伟雄教授。我们经常一起探讨诗歌翻译，吴教授总是诲人不倦，给了我莫大的鼓舞。吴教授对诗歌的热忱，以及他经常提到的许渊冲先生对诗歌的热爱，无不激励着我。

特别感谢原复旦大学教师、现美国德宝大学语言研究中心主任，汉学教授，华诗会会长，汉英双语纸质诗刊《诗殿堂》总编徐英才先生。徐教授是我诗歌翻译路上的一位导师，他博学多才、治学严谨，关爱后生学子，并写了如下评语激励我。

> 汉语是一个多韵语，同韵字相当多，这为格律诗的创作创造了有利条件。而英语是一种少韵语，同韵字相当少，因此韵译中国古诗词的难度相当大，稍不留神，译文就会流于生硬、偏离，或者基本就是那几个多韵字捣来捣去。本书译者张琼勇于直面困难，坚持采用韵译法来韵译诗歌，她的译文对原文的表达意思到位，声音和谐，常有妙笔生花处，值得一读。对现代诗的翻译，张琼努力追求诗歌的意境再造和诗歌的内在联系。她现代诗的英译自然连贯，也值得一读。

——徐英才

特别感谢中山大学王东风教授，跟随他的一年访学进修，让我受益匪浅。感谢国际学术期刊《翻译中国》的主编、上海大学赵彦春教授。

在翻译中遇到问题，赵教授马上解答，并写成博文，给了我莫大鼓舞。诗歌翻译路上，感谢《译原》电子杂志栏目主持人解斌，在其策划和主持下我进行了中国古诗词英译、中国现代诗歌英译，以及诗音画一诗多译等；感谢中诗网"双语诗界"栏目编辑王磊先生，该栏目为广大诗歌爱好者提供了诗歌交流学习平台；感谢《诗殿堂》主编，山东政法大学颜海峰副教授，副主编石永浩先生、张俊峰先生；感谢王昌玲、铁冰等诗歌译友，大家一起探讨诗歌翻译，受益良多，在此，一并致谢。

张琼

2020年1月于肇庆星湖湖畔

Preface

When James Boswell asked Samuel Johnson, "What is poetry?" Johnson answered: "Why, Sir, it is much easier to say what it is not. We all know what light is; but it is not easy to tell what it is." For a better understanding, Let's begin with reading two English poetry and my translation.

1. What Is Poetry?

By Eleanor Farjeon

What is Poetry? Who knows?
Not a rose, but the scent of the rose;
Not the sky, but the light in the sky;
Not the fly, but the gleam of the fly;
Not the sea, but the sound of the sea;
Not myself, but what makes me
See, hear, and feel something that prose
Cannot: and what it is, who knows?

1. 何为诗

埃莉诺·法杰恩

何为诗，孰知之乎？

非玫瑰，乃其香也，
非天空，乃其光也，
非萤虫，乃其亮也，
非大海，乃其声也。
非吾身，乃触吾心，
感吾耳目，而散文之不能也，
何为诗，孰知之乎？

2. Ars Poetica

By Archibald Macleish

A poem should be palpable and mute
As a globed fruit,

Dumb
As old medallions to the thumb,

Silent as the sleeve-worn stone
Of casement ledges where the moss has grown—

A poem should be wordless
As the flight of birds.

*

A poem should be motionless in time
As the moon climbs,

Leaving, as the moon releases
Twig by twig the night-entangled trees,

Leaving, as the moon behind the winter leaves,

Memory by memory the mind—

A poem should be motionless in time

As the moon climbs.

*

A poem should be equal to:

Not true.

For all the history of grief

An empty doorway and a maple leaf.

For love

The leaning grasses and two lights above the sea—

A poem should not mean

But be.

2. 诗艺

阿奇博尔德·麦克利什

诗应静默而可感知

如滚圆果子

不语

如旧奖章之于拇指

不言如衣袖磨平
的窗台石，青苔悄生——

无声
如鸟翱翔
　　　　＊
诗应静驻时光
任月攀升

隽永，任月一枝一枝
解开被黑夜纠缠的树

隽永，任月在冬身后离去
记忆于心田——

诗应静驻时光
任月攀升
　　　　＊
诗不应
写实

人生寂寥
化作空阶枫叶飘

爱意缠绵
化作芳草依依光数点——

诗不言

而是也

I loved poetry, occasionally I wrote a few lines, but the real translation of poetry had an origin. Two years ago, Professor Wu Weixiong sent me a poem and we discussed about the translation. Two days later, he asked me if I had any revision before I learned that Professor Wu had invited me to participate in translating poetry in an electronic magazine. In this way, I began to try poetry translation after years of teaching college student translation. As Professor Weng Xianliang once said: the key to the success or failure of translating foreign literary works is to gain the author's will, to use the Chinese language to achieve similar results. How can I get the author's ambition? I have followed Professor Wang Dongfeng to study of text translation, which is quite helpful. If I happen to have a question about the rhythm or rhyme of poetry, I'll discuss with Professor Wu. With the passage of time, my translated poems are published in newspapers and magazines such as China Poetry Website, *Translation of China* and *Poetry Hall*, *Journal of Zhaoqing University*, etc. Therefore, I select some of these poems with studies and assembled them into this anthology.

The great Chinese writer Mr. Lu Xun once put forward the theory of "three aesthetic principles" about Chinese literature creation: "Meaning for the heart, sound for the ear, form for the eye." (general meaning, my translation) Professor Xu Yuanchong transplanted Lu Xun's "three aesthetic principles" to poetry translation based on his own practice of translating poetry. In Mr. Xu Yuanchong's view, in the process of translating poetry, the pursuit of "truth" and "beauty" does not conflict, the pursuit of beauty also preserves the truth of the original poem to a certain extent. Poetry pursues beauty, and translation pursues truth. Poetry has no exegesis, and translation has no definite method. The translation of poetry is a regrettable art. As Mr. Tu'an said, no matter how faithful the translator is to the original, there is always a distance between the translation and the original, and a 100% authentic translation of poetry does not exist. It is said American poet Frost once said "poetry is what gets lost in translation", which means translation of poetry is always an imperfect art.

In the process of poetry translation, we try to follow the rhythm and rhyme of the original poetry besides the meaning, sometimes even punctuation, as far as possible consistent with the original poem. We pursue the exact meaning of the original poem, clear, fluent natural expression with few notes. We try to find a balance point in the continuum of "seeking truth" and "seeking beauty". Let's illustrate with two or three examples.

"Spring Day" is a poem written by Zhu Xi, a thinker and educator in the Song Dynasty. It seems that literally the poem is a simple landscape poem, depicting the beautiful scenery of spring; in fact, it is a philosophical poem, expressing the poet's good desire to pursue the way of the Saint Confucius in troubled times. The conception of the poem is full of images. In translating this classical Chinese poem, we adopt the iambic pentameter and follow the rhyme format aabb. The original and translated poems are as follows.

3. 春日

〔宋〕朱熹

胜日寻芳泗水滨,
无边光景一时新。
等闲识得东风面,

万紫千红总是春。

3. Spring Day
By Zhu Xi

I'm seeking scenes by Si River on a sunny day:
Grass lush, flowers blooming, a thriving way.
Refreshed by a sudden breath of spring in air,
I see in myriads of colors spring hide there.

The free verse in modern times is written in natural rhythm with abundant images, which cares little about rhyme. *Lunar September* written by Haizi is a typical free verse with a tone extremely painful, full of mysterious atmosphere, ethereal time and broad space kink entangled together, life and death in the interpretation of each other. In the translation of this poem, we try to experience and reproduce the poet's feelings. With the images of "prairie" "wild flowers" "wind" "horse-head qin" "moon", the poet creates a melancholy autumn. In the translation, we focus on the poeticity besides the meaning. The original poem and translation are as follows.

4. 九月
海子

目击众神死亡的草原上野花一片
远在远方的风比远方更远
我的琴声呜咽 泪水全无
我把这远方的远归还草原

一个叫马头 一个叫马尾
我的琴声呜咽 泪水全无

远方只有在死亡中凝聚野花一片
明月如镜高悬草原映照千年岁月
我的琴声呜咽 泪水全无
只身打马过草原

4. Lunar September

By Haizi

The prairie witnessed the death of pantheon presents boundless wild flowers

The wind afar is even farther away from afar

My strings sob with tearless grief

I return to the prairie the afar from afar

One is called horse-head, the other horse-tail

My strings sob with tearless grief

The afar only in death converges a sheet of wild flowers

The mirror-like moon hangs high over the land reflecting time of thousands of years

My strings sob with tearless grief

Alone I ride a horse across the prairie

Rhythm is the breath of a poetry, here is another example below. "*A Bird Came down the Walk*" is iambic trimeter poem with some variation. The whole poem is divided into 5 verses, 4 lines each, with only one full stop, which is a complete and coherent animation. Dickinson sketched the image of "bird" with concise strokes in a series of movements (came down, bit, ate, drank, hopped, glanced, stirred, unrolled, rowed), while she hid herself in the background (e. g. I saw, I thought). Later, "my" intervention (e. g. I offered) disturbed the peace of the bird. As a result, the bird spread its wings and flew away. "Dun" is a pause according to the meaning group in Chinese poetry, which is not equivalent to foot in English poetry, but can be used to express the rhythm of the English poetry in a certain extend in E-C poetry translation. In the translation of this poem, we adopt "Dun" to create the same effect of the original rhythm and follow the same punctuation to reproduce the rhythm of whole poetic picture. The rhythm analysis of the original poem and my translation are as follows.

5. A Bird Came down the Walk
By Emily Dickinson

A Bird /came down /the Walk—
He did/ not know /I saw—
He bit/ an Ang/le Worm/ in halves
And ate /the fel/low, raw,

And then/ he drank /a Dew
From a /conve/nient Grass—
And then/ hopped side/wise to /the Wall
To let/ a Bee/tle pass—

He glanced /with rap/id eyes
That hur/ried all /around—

They looked /like fright/ened Beads, /I thought—
He stirred/ his Vel/vet Head

Like one/ in danger, / Cautious,
I of/fered him/ a Crumb
And he/ unro/lled his /feathers
And rowed/ him sof/ter home—

Than Oars /divide /the Ocean,
Too sil/ver for /a seam—
Or But/terflies, /off Banks /of Noon
Leap, / plashless /as they swim.

5. 小鸟沿小径走来
[美]艾米莉·狄金森

小鸟/沿小径/走来——
不知/一旁/我在瞧——
他把/一条/蚯蚓/啄开
再吃掉/那家伙, /生嚼,

他将/清露/饮吞
取自/近旁/草叶上——
又侧身/跳到/旁边/墙脚根
来给/甲虫/把路让——

急促地/左顾/右盼
他那/滴溜溜的/眼眸——

活像/受惊的/珠子,/我想——
见他/抖了抖/毛茸茸的头

好像/身处险境,/十分小心,
我给他/分点/碎面包
而他/立刻/展开/羽翎
往回/飞去/一路轻飘——

胜过/船桨/划海面,
波光/银白/水无痕——
胜过/蝴蝶,/晌午/草埂边
跃下,/游弋/无溅声。

Lakeside Poetic Breeze: *English Translation of 100 Classic Chinese Poems*, *Lakeside Poetic Sense*: *English Translation of 100 Contemporary Chinese Poems*, and *Lakeside Poetic Bridge*: *100 Poems Translated Between Chinese and English* are a series of poetry translation studies. In this book, 100 classic Chinese poems before the Qing Dynasty are selected and arranged according to the order of the dynasty. Some of the translated poems have been published in the electronic journals and print media and revised in this book. This book is suitable for college English majors and non-English majors, English teachers, poetry lovers and poetry translators.

  Poetry and poetry translation have improved my perceptual quality and aesthetic taste, enriched my life experience and cognition, and made me spiritually happy. In this poetry translation way, I appreciate all those who have cared, helped and inspired me. First of all, I would like to thank Professor Wu Weixiong from Zhuhai Institute of Technology, Beijing

Institute of Technology. We often discuss poetry translation together, and Professor Wu has given me great encouragement. Professor Wu's enthusiasm for poetry as well as his often mention of Mr. Xu Yuanchong's love of poetry, all inspired me.

I would like to express my warmest thanks to Mr. Xu Yingcai, former Fudan University teacher, Professor of Sinology in the Language Department of Depaul University, President of the Chinese Poetry Society, and Editor-in-chief of the Chinese-English bilingual journal *Poetry Hall*. Professor Xu is a good teacher on my way of poetry translation. He is knowledgeable, rigorous and caring. He writes the following comments to inspire me:

> Chinese is a rhyme-rich language with a broad spectrum of shared syllables, which facilitates an easy writing of rhyming poetry, while English is a rhyme-poor language with quite limited number of similar syllables, which creates a great difficulty for rhyme-translating traditional Chinese poetry. Therefore, rhyme-translating traditional Chinese poems tends to be effortful in wording, disloyal to the original, and repeated use of the very few rhyming friendly syllables. However, in translating this anthology of classical Chinese poems, Zhang Qiong confronts the difficulty and insists in rhyme translating. Her translation conveys the meaning of the original with harmonious rhymes and rhythms, and often blossoms. Her translation is a rewarding reading. In the translation of modern poetry, Zhang Qiong makes every effort to recreate the poetic imagery and inner coherence. Her translation is natural and coherent, which is worth reading too.
>
> ——Xu Yingcai

I would also like to thank Professor Wang Dongfeng of Sun Yat-sen University for a year's translation study guided by him. Thanks go to Professor Zhao Yanchun, Editor-in-Chief of the International Academic Journal *Translating China*. When I had a question about poetry translation, Professor Zhao immediately answered and wrote a blog, which gave me great encouragement. I would also give thanks to Mr. Xie Bin, column host of *Yiyuan Electronic Magazine*, Mr. Wang Lei, column host of *Translation of Chinese Poetry to Foreign Versions* and *Translation of Foreign Poetry to Chinese Version* in China Poetry Website. Thanks also go to my editorial colleagues Mr. Yan Haifeng, associate professor of Shandong University of Political Science and Law; Mr. Shi Yonghao, associate professor of Shandong University of Political Science and Law; Mr. Zhang Junfeng, English teacher of USST; my peer poetry translator Ms. Wang Changling and Mr. Iceiron. We have been discussing the translation of poetry together, which benefits me a lot.

Zhang Qiong
Jan. 2020 by Star Lake, Zhaoqing

目　录/Content

1. 关雎 ·· 001
    Cooing and Wooing ··· 002
2. 咏春风诗 ··· 004
    Ode to Spring Breeze ·· 004
3. 长歌行 ··· 005
    A Song in Slow Time ··· 005
4. 七步诗 ··· 007
    A Poem Finished in Seven Steps ························· 007
5. 山中问答 ··· 009
    A Dialogue in the Hills ·· 009
6. 静夜思 ··· 011
    Nostalgia on a Tranquil Night ······························ 011
7. 赠汪伦 ··· 012
    To Wang Lun ··· 012
8. 夜宿山寺 ··· 014
    An Overnight Stay in Alpine Temple ···················· 014
9. 独坐敬亭山 ·· 016
    Sitting Alone in Mount Jingting ··························· 016
10. 夏日山中 ·· 018
    A Summer Day in the Hill ···································· 018

11. 望庐山瀑布 ·· 020
   Cataract at Mt. Lushan Viewed Afar ·················· 020

12. 望天门山 ·· 022
   Mount Heaven's Gate Viewed Afar ···················· 022

13. 黄鹤楼送孟浩然之广陵 ································ 024
   Seeing Meng Haoran off at Yellow Crane Tower ··· 024

14. 秋浦歌 ·· 026
   A Song in Qiupu ·· 026

15. 绝句 ··· 028
   A Quatrain ·· 028

16. 春夜喜雨 ·· 030
   Timely Rain on a Spring Night ························ 030

17. 九月九日忆山东兄弟 ··································· 032
   Missing My Brothers on Double Ninth Festival ··· 032

18. 山居秋暝 ·· 034
   Autumn Dusk in Mountains ···························· 034

19. 画 ·· 036
   A Painting ·· 036

20. 送元二使安西 ··· 038
   A Farewell Song ·· 038

21. 鹿柴 ··· 040
   The Deer Enclosure ······································ 040

22. 相思 ··· 042
   Love Seeds ··· 042

23. 黄鹤楼 ·· 044
   Yellow Crane Tower ······································ 044

24. 忆江南 · · · · · · 046
   A Wisp of Memory of the Southern Shore · · · · · · 046
25. 草 · · · · · · 048
   Grass on the Ancient Plain · · · · · · 048
26. 借问江潮与海水 · · · · · · 050
   May I Ask Sea Water and River Tides · · · · · · 050
27. 苦热题恒寂师禅室 · · · · · · 052
   A Poem to Zen Master Hengji Written on His Meditation Wall in Dog Days · · · · · · 052
28. 重阳席上赋白菊 · · · · · · 054
   Ode to the White Chrysanthemums on Double Ninth Festival · · · · · · 054
29. 惜牡丹花 · · · · · · 056
   Poor Peony · · · · · · 056
30. 池上 · · · · · · 057
   On the Pool · · · · · · 057
31. 大林寺桃花 · · · · · · 058
   Peach Blossoms in the Temple of Great Forest · · · · · · 058
32. 暮江吟 · · · · · · 060
   Chant to Twilight River · · · · · · 060
33. 咏鹅 · · · · · · 062
   Ode to Goose · · · · · · 062
34. 咏柳 · · · · · · 064
   Ode to the Willow · · · · · · 064
35. 回乡偶书 · · · · · · 066
   A Whim About Home-Coming · · · · · · 066
36. 登幽州台歌 · · · · · · 068
   On the Tower of Youzhou · · · · · · 068

37. 题都城南庄 ·· 070
    Written in a Village Southern of the Capital ·············· 070
38. 江雪 ·· 072
    Fishing Snow ··· 072
39. 清明 ·· 074
    Qingming Festival ···································· 074
40. 山行 ·· 076
    A Mountain Trip ····································· 076
41. 望洞庭 ·· 078
    Lake Dongting Viewed Afar ··························· 078
42. 秋词 ·· 080
    Ode to Autumn ······································ 080
43. 八至 ·· 082
    Eight Extremes ······································ 082
44. 一七令·茶 ·· 084
    Song of One to Seven Words · Tea ····················· 084
45. 凉州词 ·· 086
    Liangzhou Song ······································ 086
46. 桃花溪 ·· 088
    Peach Blossom Brook ································ 088
47. 望月怀远 ·· 090
    Yearning Under the Moon ···························· 090
48. 西江夜行 ·· 092
    The Night Voyage on Xijiang River ··················· 092
49. 感遇·其一 ·· 094
    An Epiphany · Poem One ····························· 094

50. 登鹳雀楼 ·· 096
   Ascending the Stork Tower ······················· 096
51. 瑶池 ·· 098
   Jade Pool ·· 098
52. 春晓 ·· 100
   Spring Dawn ··· 100
53. 初秋 ·· 102
   Early Autumn ·· 102
54. 渡浙江问舟中人 ···································· 103
   Asking the Peers While Crossing the Qiantang River ······ 103
55. 菊花 ·· 105
   Chrysanthemums ···································· 105
56. 菩提偈 ··· 107
   Bodhi Verse ·· 107
57. 回归自我 ··· 108
   Return Back to Who I Am ························ 108
58. 渔歌子 ··· 110
   A Fisherman's Song ································ 110
59. 以退为进 ··· 112
   Regressing to Progress ···························· 112
60. 梅 ··· 114
   Plum Blossom ······································· 114
61. 泊船瓜洲 ··· 116
   Moored at Melon Islet ···························· 116
62. 饮湖上初晴后雨 ···································· 118
   Drinking on Lake, Sunny First Then Rainy ······ 118

005

63. 赠刘景文 ·· 120
   To Liu Jingwen ···································· 120
64. 题西林壁 ·· 122
   A Poem Inscribed on the Wall of Xilin Temple ········ 122
65. 定风波·莫听穿林打叶声 ···························· 124
   Calming the Waves · Listen Not to the Rain Pattering the Leaves ··· 124
66. 山村咏怀 ·· 126
   A Lyric of a Mountain Village ························ 126
67. 生查子·元夕 ··· 127
   Song of Hawthorn · Lantern Festival ················· 127
68. 虞美人·寄公度 ······································ 129
   Beautiful Lady Yu · To My Friend, Gongdu ·········· 129
69. 长相思·吴山青 ······································ 131
   Everlasting Longing · Wu Hills Green ················ 131
70. 一剪梅·红藕香残玉簟秋 ···························· 133
   A Twig of Plum Blossoms · Lotus Flowers Fade, Bamboo Mats Cold ··· 133
71. 夏日绝句 ·· 135
   A Quatrain in Summer ······························· 135
72. 如梦令·昨夜雨疏风骤 ······························ 137
   A Dreamy Song · The Wind Whistled with Little Rain Last Night ····· 137
73. 夜书所见 ·· 139
   Nostalgia Sights on a Lonely Night ·················· 139
74. 初秋 ·· 141
   Early Autumn ·· 141
75. 除夜雪 ··· 143
   Snow on New Year's Eve ··························· 143

76. 游山西村 ·· 145
　　A Visit to the Village of Shanxi ·············· 145
77. 示儿 ·· 147
　　To My Son ··· 147
78. 春日 ·· 149
　　Spring Day ·· 149
79. 观书有感 ·· 151
　　Reflections on the Book ······················· 151
80. 拒霜 ·· 152
　　Cotton Rose ······································· 152
81. 清平乐·村居 ······································· 155
　　Pure Serene Music · Village Life ············ 155
82. 西江月·夜行黄沙道中 ·························· 157
　　The Moon over the West River · A Night Walk on Huangsha Road ······ 157
83. 小池 ·· 159
　　A Small Pond ····································· 159
84. 晓出净慈寺送林子方 ···························· 161
　　Seeing off My Friend at Lakeside Temple at Dawn ·············· 161
85. 宿新市徐公店 ······································ 163
　　An Overnight Stay at the Xu's Inn ········· 163
86. 夏夜追凉 ·· 165
　　Seeking Cool on Summer Night ············ 165
87. 舟过安仁 ·· 167
　　Going by Anren on Boat ······················ 167
88. 乡村四月 ·· 169
　　Late Spring in the Countryside ·············· 169

007

89. 丙申元旦守母制因感而作 ·· 171
    Sentiments on the Lunar New Year in Observing Mourning for My Mother ········ 171
90. 天净沙·秋 ··· 173
    Clear Sand · Autumn ··· 173
91. 画鸡 ··· 175
    A Painting of a Rooster ··· 175
92. 次韵陆金宪元日春晴 ··· 177
    Spring Clear, Written According to the Rhyming Words of New Year's Day by Lu Qianxian ········ 177
93. 临江仙 ··· 179
    Riverside Daffodils ··· 179
94. 长相思 ··· 181
    Everlasting Yearning ·· 181
95. 村居 ··· 183
    A Village Scene ··· 183
96. 绮怀诗 ··· 185
    Love Is but a Dream ··· 185
97. 对月寓怀 ··· 187
    A Lyric to the Full Moon ·· 187
98. 山中雪后 ··· 189
    The Hill-Scene After Snow ·· 189
99. 惠州西湖玩月 ·· 191
    Admiring the Moon by Lake ·· 191
100. 《儒林外史》中的一首宝塔诗 ··· 192
    A shape poem in The Scholars ······································· 192

参考文献 ··· 194

1. 关雎

〔先秦〕无名氏

关关雎鸠,
在河之洲。
窈窕淑女,
君子好逑。

参差荇菜,
左右流之。
窈窕淑女,
寤寐求之。

求之不得,
寤寐思服。
悠哉悠哉,
辗转反侧。

参差荇菜,
左右采之。
窈窕淑女,
琴瑟友之。

参差荇菜,
左右芼之。
窈窕淑女,
钟鼓乐之。

1. *Cooing and Wooing*

〔the Pre-Qin Period〕Anonymous

Coo, coo, on the sandbar,
Sing a pair of turtle-doves.
The lass at riverside not far
Is the youngster' ideal love.

Fringed water lilies, long or short,
The lass picks some left and right.
The fair lass, adored and courted,
The lad yearns for her day and night.

He woos her, but she flees;
Fantasies creep upon his mind.
Toss and turn, he cannot sleep,
Giving sighs a whole night!

Water lilies, fresh and tender;
The fair lass, sweet and slender.
Ballads and ditties are played;
The nice lad woos his date.

Water lilies, fresh and tender;

The fair lass, sweet and slender.
Bells and drums are played;
The nice lad marries his mate.

译后小记

《关雎》这一首诗篇写"君子"对"淑女"的追求，此诗在艺术上巧妙地采用了"兴"的表现手法。首章以雎鸟相向合鸣，相依相恋，兴起淑女配君子的联想。以下各章，又以采荇菜这一行为兴起主人公对女子疯狂地相思与追求。全诗语言优美，善于运用双声、叠韵和重叠词，增强了诗歌的音韵美和写人状物、拟声传情的生动性。

"关关"是雎鸠的叫声，雎鸠是水鸟，经常栖息于湖水边，如鸳鸯一般生活，故古人将其视为男女相恋的象征。故将"关关"译为 coo, coo，"雎鸠"译为 turtle dove。

"荇菜"，别称莕菜、莲叶莕菜、驴蹄菜、水荷叶，叶片形睡莲，小巧别致，鲜黄色花朵挺出水面，花多且花期长，是庭院点缀水景的佳品，根据图片，找到对应英文为 fringed water lily。

翻译此诗，译者追求语义流畅，音韵和谐。题目译为 Cooing and Wooing，一是雎鸠的叫声，一是"君子"对"淑女"的追求；原诗五节，每节四句，译诗按照原诗节律，前三节采用尾韵 abab，后两节押尾韵 aabb；有行中头韵，如 toss and turn，有行中腹韵，如 adored and courted, fresh and tender。

2. 咏春风诗

〔南梁〕何逊

可闻不可见，
能重复能轻。
镜前飘落粉，
琴上响余声。

2. *Ode to Spring Breeze*

〔Liang Dynasty〕By He Xun

You're in my ears but not sight,
With steps either heavy or light,
With dust floated onto the glass,
Tinkling, tinkling as you pass.

译后小记

此诗像一谜语，诗人歌咏春风，文中却不着"风"字，将风写得如此生动。原诗是无主句，英语必须有主语，译诗将风拟人化，采用 you 为主语，似乎"你"走过留下或轻或重的"脚步"；追求连贯流畅，"tinkling, tinkling"是"琴上响余声"化作具体声响。

译诗行尾押完全韵，格式为 aabb。

3. 长歌行

汉乐府民歌

佚名

青青园中葵,
朝露待日晞。
阳春布德泽,
万物生光辉。
常恐秋节至,
焜黄华叶衰。
百川东到海,
何时复西归。
少壮不努力,
老大徒伤悲。

3. *A Song in Slow Time*

Folk Songs in the Han Dynasty

Anonymous

Lush mallows in garden are green
With dews await the sunbeams.
The spring brings rain and sunshine;
All things are teemed with life.
The coming of autumn, I fear,

Will make leaves yellow grass sere.
All rivers flowing east to sea
Will never return west, you see.
If you idle your youth away,
Regrets will be on your way.

译后小记

汉乐府民歌,在我国诗歌史上,是继《诗经》《楚辞》之后出现的第三个重要发展阶段。它以现实主义的创作方法真实地反映了汉代广阔的社会生活和人民的思想感情。

此诗借物言理,从"园中葵"说起,以园中的葵菜作比喻,"青青"喻其生长茂盛。"阳春布德泽,万物生光辉。"春天把阳光、雨露带给万物,万物都呈现出一派繁荣。整个春天的阳光雨露之下,万物都在争相努力地生长,因为它们都恐怕秋天很快地到来,深知秋风凋零百草的道理。再用水流入海不复回打比方,说明光阴如流水,一去不再回。最后劝导人们,要珍惜青春年华,发奋努力,不要等老了再后悔。诗歌由对宇宙的探寻转入对人生的思考,终于推出"少壮不努力,老大徒伤悲"这一发聋振聩的结论,结束全诗。

翻译接近原诗风格,行尾押不完全韵,押韵格式为 aabbccddee,基本上每两行一句为一个完整句子。

4. 七步诗

〔三国〕曹植

煮豆燃豆萁,
豆在釜中泣。
本是同根生,
相煎何太急?

4. A Poem Finished in Seven Steps

〔the Three Kingdoms〕By Cao Zhi

Beans are boiled by burning beanstalk;
In the pot the beans weep and squawk:
"We were born in the same root of pea,
Why are you so eager to cook me?"

译后小记

据《世说新语·文学》记载:"文帝(曹丕)尝令东阿王(曹植)七步中作诗,不成者行大法(杀),应声便为诗……帝深有惭色。"(曹植的哥哥曹丕做了皇帝后,要想迫害曹植,以曹植未能及时吊唁先父为由认为其大不孝,于是命令曹植在走七步路的时间内作一首诗,作不成就杀头。结果曹植应声咏出这首《七步诗》,曹丕感到十分羞愧)。据说曹丕听了以后"深有惭色"不仅因为曹植在咏诗中体现了非凡的才华,具有出口成章的本领，使得文帝自觉不如，而且由于诗中以浅显生动的比喻说明兄弟本为手足，不应互相猜忌与怨恨，晓之以大义，自然令文帝羞愧万分，无地自容。

此诗纯以比兴的手法出之，语言浅显，寓意明畅。翻译"泣"用了weep and squawk（哭哭啼啼，哭着说），squawk 正好与 beanstalk 押韵；然后带出后两句，译诗采用直接引语，情景直观呈现。原诗押韵方式为东方韵 aaba，译诗押韵方式为联韵 aabb。

5. 山中问答

〔唐〕李白

问余何意栖碧山,
笑而不答心自闲。
桃花流水窅然去,
别有天地非人间。

5. *A Dialogue in the Hills*

〔Tang Dynasty〕By Li Bai

You ask me why I inhabit in green hills?
I greet you with silence in a delight smile.
Peach blossoms are flowing away on rills
To a wonderland which worth my while.

译后小记

《山中问答》是唐代伟大诗人李白的作品。这是一首古绝,以问答形式抒发作者隐居生活的自在天然的情趣,也反映了诗人的矛盾心理。全诗语言朴素,转接轻灵,活泼流利,浑然天成;用笔有虚有实,实处形象可感,虚处一触即止,虚实对比,意蕴幽邃;诗境似近而实远,诗情似淡而实浓。

第一联:"问余何意栖碧山,笑而不答心自闲。"前句起得突兀,后句接得迷离。诗以提问的形式领起，突出题旨，以唤起读者的注意。当人们正要倾听答案时，诗人笔锋却故意一晃，"笑而不答"。第二联："桃花流水窅然去，别有天地非人间。"这是写"碧山"之景，其实也就是"何意栖碧山"的答案。这种"不答"而答、似断实连的结构，加深了诗的韵味。

这首诗完全是口语体，语言朴素，似行云流水，流畅自然，浑然天成。全诗虽然只有四句二十八字，但是有问、有答，有叙述、有描绘、有议论。

在理解原诗的基础上，译诗贴近原诗风格译出，行尾押完全韵，押韵格式为交韵 abab。最后一行，译诗似乎多加了"which worth my while"，其实语意连贯，译出原文，后两句连起来为 Peach blossoms are flowing away on rills／To a wonderland which worth my while。(桃花在小溪上流淌，流向一个值得我花时间的仙境)

6. 静夜思

〔唐〕李白

床前明月光，
疑是地上霜。
举头望明月，
低头思故乡。

6. *Nostalgia on a Tranquil Night*

〔Tang Dynasty〕By Li Bai

Abed is a pool of moonlight,
Is that frost? I think it might.
Head up, I see the moon,
Head down, I miss my home.

译后小记

《静夜思》是唐代诗人李白所作的一首五言古诗。此诗描写了秋日夜晚，诗人于屋内抬头望月的所感。诗中运用比喻、衬托等手法，表达客居思乡之情，语言清新朴素而韵味含蓄无穷，历来广为传诵。

"静夜思"，安静的夜晚产生的思绪，故译为 Nostalgia on a Tranquil Night。此诗中的"床"字，是争论和异议的焦点，译诗主要关注意境，不作深入探讨。译诗旨在流畅、自然地表达原诗诗意。

7. 赠汪伦

〔唐〕李白

李白乘舟将欲行，
忽闻岸上踏歌声。
桃花潭水深千尺，
不及汪伦送我情。

7. *To Wang Lun*

〔Tang Dynasty〕By Li Bai

The moment I am on boat to go,
I hear your farewell songlet flow.
Peach Pool is a thousand feet deep,
Yet not deep as your friendship to me.

译后小记

《赠汪伦》是唐代大诗人李白游历桃花潭时写给当地好友汪伦的一首留别诗。全诗语言清新自然，想象丰富奇特，虽仅四句二十八字，却是李白诗中流传最广的佳作之一。

诗的前半部分是叙事，描写的是送别的场面。起句先写李白正要离去，次句继写送行者。此句不像首句那样直叙，而用了曲笔，只说听见"踏歌声"。译诗用 the moment 将这两句连接起来，再现此情此景。

诗的后半部分是抒情。第三句遥接起句，进一步说明放船地点在桃花潭。"深千尺"既描绘了潭的特点，又为结句预伏一笔。桃花潭水是那样深湛，更触动了离人的情怀，难忘汪伦的深情厚意，水深情深自然地联系起来。结句迸出"不及汪伦送我情"，潭水已"深千尺"，那么汪伦送李白的情谊必定更深，此句耐人寻味。妙就妙在"不及"二字，好就好在不用比喻而采用比物手法，变无形的情谊为生动的形象，空灵而有余味，自然而又情真。"深千尺"是夸张手法，虚指，译诗直译为 a thousand feet deep，不必纠结"尺"与 feet 之间的差别，但还是不及你的情谊(Yet It's not deep as your friendship for me)。

8. 夜宿山寺

〔唐〕李白

危楼高百尺,
手可摘星辰。
不敢高声语,
恐惊天上人。

8. *An Overnight Stay in Alpine Temple*

〔Tang Dynasty〕By Li Bai

The tower seems one hundred feet high;
One could reach out to pluck stars nigh.
We all hushed our voices in whispers,
Lest we should disturb the dwellers in sky.

译后小记

《夜宿山寺》运用了极其夸张的手法,描写了寺中楼宇的高耸,表达了诗人对古代庙宇工程艺术的惊叹以及对神仙般生活的向往和追求之情。全诗语言朴素自然,想象瑰丽,夸张巧妙,活灵活现,给人以丰富的联想和身临其境之感。

首句正面描绘寺楼的峻峭挺拔、高耸入云。发端一个"危"字,倍显突兀醒目,与"高"字在同句中的巧妙组合,就确切、生动、形象地将山寺屹立山巅、雄视寰宇的非凡气势淋漓尽致地描摹了出来。"危"亦是突出"高",译者合而译之,用 one hundred feet high 来表达。

次句以极其夸张的技法来烘托山寺之高耸云霄,以星夜的美丽引起人们对高耸入云的"危楼"的向往。译诗以虚拟语气译出这种夸张表达。

三四两句,"不敢"写出了作者夜临"危楼"时的心理状态,从诗人"不敢"与"恐惊"的心理中,读者完全可以想象到"山寺"与"天上人"的相距之近,这样,山寺之高也就不言自明了。"不敢高声语,恐惊天上人",译诗换一个视角,用虚拟语气来表达,以求异曲同工之妙。

译诗采用东方韵 aaba。

9. 独坐敬亭山

〔唐〕李白

众鸟高飞尽,
孤云独去闲。
相看两不厌,
只有敬亭山。

9. *Sitting Alone in Mount Jingting*

〔Tang Dynasty〕By Li Bai

Birds fly high and out of sight,
And a lonely cloud idles by.
Gazing at each other, never tied,
Are only Mount. Jingting and I.

译后小记

《独坐敬亭山》是诗人表现自己精神世界的佳作。此诗表面是写独游敬亭山的情趣,而其深含之意则是诗人生命历程中旷世的孤独感。诗人以奇特的想象力和巧妙的构思,赋予山水景物以生命,将敬亭山拟人化,写得十分生动。作者写的是自己的孤独和自己的怀才不遇,但更是自己的坚定,在大自然中寻求安慰和寄托。

此诗前两句"众鸟高飞尽,孤云独去闲",看似写眼前之景,其实,把伤心之感写尽了：天上几只鸟儿高飞远去，直至无影无踪；寥廓的长空还有一片白云，却也不愿停留，慢慢地越飘越远，似乎世间万物都在厌弃诗人。"尽""闲"两个字，把读者引入一个"静"的境界。译诗中 birds，鸟的复数，即是"众鸟"。

三四两句"相看两不厌，只有敬亭山"用浪漫主义手法，将敬亭山人格化、个性化。尽管鸟飞云去，诗人仍没有回去，也不想回去，他久久地凝望着幽静秀丽的敬亭山，觉得敬亭山似乎也正含情脉脉地看着他自己。他们之间不必说什么话，已达到了感情上的交流。这里是拟人化的描写，译者用 gazing at each other 来表达，三四句为倒装句，never tied 作插入语，补充说明。

译诗隔行押韵 abab。

这首诗的翻译，笔者还有"百人百译"评比第一的版本，一气呵成，行尾押抱韵，更显诗人的惆怅之感，具体如下：

> Birds fly high and out of sight,
> And then a lonely cloud idles by,
> Leaving Mount Jingting and I,
> Face to face from day to night.

10. 夏日山中

〔唐〕李白

懒摇白羽扇,
裸袒青林中。
脱巾挂石壁,
露顶洒松风。

10. *A Summer Day in the Hill*

〔Tang Dynasty〕By Li Bai

I don't bother to shake a white feather fan
With my chest and back exposed at ease.
Taking the hat off, I hang it on the rock;
My bare head enjoys the pine breeze.

译后小记

《夏日山中》是唐代浪漫主义诗人唐代李白创作的一首五言绝句。诗中描写的夏日中生活的场景,真实、贴切地展现了夏日山中和山中夏日的景象。

"懒摇白羽扇,裸袒青林中。"因为是夏天,所以有"白羽扇";因为是山中,所以有扇而懒得摇。因为山林中人烟稀少,诗人敢于脱去头巾,表现出悠然自得,不拘礼法的形象。句中通过"懒""裸"突出了诗人在山中夏日乘凉的悠闲情趣，描绘了一幅生动的夏日消闲图画。"懒"译为 I don't bother，意为"不必费神去……"；"白羽扇"译为 a white feather fan，押头韵。

"脱巾挂石壁，露顶洒松风。"诗人解下头巾，挂在山中的石壁上，多么凉爽宜人。袒胸露顶，栖身林下，大有解除尘累，反归自然的情趣。通过"脱""露"来表达诗人无拘无束，向往自然的心情。"脱""露"，译者用了两个现在分词 taking off 和 hanging on 表示，紧接主句 My bare head enjoys the pine breeze（我光秃秃的头享受着松树林的微风，好不惬意）。

译诗二、四句行尾 ease 与 breeze 押完全韵。

11. 望庐山瀑布

〔唐〕李白

日照香炉生紫烟,
遥看瀑布挂前川。
飞流直下三千尺,
疑是银河落九天。

11. *Cataract at Mt. Lushan Viewed Afar*

〔Tang Dynasty〕By Li Bai

The sun shines on Peak and violet mist flows;
Seen afar, the cataract on the Mount glows.
Dashing down three thousand feet from high,
As if Silver River is falling from the ninth sky.

译后小记

《望庐山瀑布》是诗人五十岁左右隐居庐山时,创作的七言绝句。这首诗形象地描绘了庐山瀑布雄奇壮丽的景色,反映了诗人对祖国大好河山的无限热爱。

首句"日照香炉生紫烟"。"香炉"是指庐山的香炉峰,由于瀑布飞泻,水汽蒸腾而上,在丽日照耀下,仿佛有座顶天立地的香炉冉冉升起了团团紫烟。译者用 shines 来译日"照",用 flows 来译烟"生"。

次句"遥看瀑布挂前川"。"遥看瀑布"四字照应了题目《望庐山瀑布》。"挂"字化动为静,"挂前川"是说瀑布像一条巨大的白练挂在山前。远远望去,瀑布在阳光下应该是闪亮的,故译为 Seen afar, the cataract on the Mount glows。

第三句"飞流直下三千尺","飞"字把瀑布喷涌而出的景象描绘得极为生动;"直下"既写出山之高峻陡峭,又可以见出水流之急,那高空直落,势不可挡之状如在眼前。译诗用 dashing down 来译"飞流直下","三千英尺"(three thousand feet)与"三千尺",异曲同工。

第四句"疑是银河落九天"这一比喻,虽是奇特,但在诗中并不是凭空而来,而是在形象的刻画中自然地生发出来的,译为 As if the Silver River is falling from the ninth sky。中国传统说天有九霄,"九重天"是数量词,"九重天"中的"九"字,只是因为它是数字单数中最大的数字,所以有"极限"之意,这里直译。

译诗行尾押联韵 aabb。

12. 望天门山

〔唐〕李白

天门中断楚江开，
碧水东流至此回。
两岸青山相对出，
孤帆一片日边来。

12. *Mount Heaven's Gate Viewed Afar*

〔Tang Dynasty〕By Li Bai

Bursting the Heaven's Gate, the River roars severe;
The blue river flowing eastward turns north here.
Green mountains on both sides thrust out near;
Leaving the sun behind, a sail moves along there.

译后小记

《望天门山》是唐代大诗人李白于开元十三年（725年）赴江东途中行至天门山时所创作的一首七绝。此诗描写了诗人舟行江中顺流而下远望天门山的情景：前两句用铺叙的方法，描写天门山的雄奇壮观和江水浩荡奔流的气势；后两句描绘出从两岸青山夹缝中望过去的远景，显示了一种动态美。

诗的前两句即从"江"与"山"的关系着笔。第一句"天门中断楚江开",紧扣题目,总写天门山,着重写出浩荡东流的楚江冲破天门山奔腾而去的壮阔气势。翻译时,考虑字数限制,"天门(山)"译为 the Heaven's Gate,"楚江"译为 the River,在诗中上下文语境也不会有歧义。为再现江水的气势,选了两个词 bursting 和 roars 来表达。第二句"碧水东流至此回",反过来写夹江对峙的天门山对汹涌奔腾的楚江的约束力和反作用。"碧水"是第二句的主语,"东流"在译诗化作定语,"至此回"作谓语,于是整句译为 The blue river flowing eastward turns north here。

"两岸青山相对出,孤帆一片日边来。"这两句是一个不可分割的整体。"两岸青山相对出"的"出"字,使本来静止不动的山带上了动态美,因为诗人站在从"日边来"的"一片孤帆"来观看天门山。译诗也从诗人视角来译。

13. 黄鹤楼送孟浩然之广陵

〔唐〕李白

故人西辞黄鹤楼，
烟花三月下扬州。
孤帆远影碧空尽，
唯见长江天际流。

13. *Seeing Meng Haoran off at Yellow Crane Tower*

〔Tang Dynasty〕By Li Bai

My friend bids farewell at Yellow Crane Tower
To Yangzhou in green willows and red flowers.
In blue blankness disappears the lonely boat;
I can only see the rolling River to horizon flow.

译后小记

《黄鹤楼送孟浩然之广陵》是唐代大诗人李白创作的一首送别诗。

首句点出送别的地点：一代名胜黄鹤楼；二句写送别的时间与去向："烟花三月"和东南形胜的"扬州"；三四句写送别的场景：目送孤帆远去，只留一江春水。

第二句"烟花三月"的"烟"，这一意象具体说法不一。古诗词里多指以柳树为代表的"春烟",如高鼎的"草长莺飞二月天,拂堤杨柳醉春烟",王维的"桃红复含宿雨,柳绿更带春烟",故译者将这里的"烟花"意象具体化,译为"green willows and red flowers"。

"孤帆远影碧空尽,惟见长江天际流。"诗的后两句看起来似乎是写景,但在写景中包含着一个充满诗意的细节。诗人目送远去的风帆,一直看到帆影逐渐模糊,消失在碧空的尽头(In blue blankness disappears the lonely boat),这才注意到一江春水,在浩浩荡荡地流向远远的水天交接之处(I can only see the rolling River to horizon flow)。

14. 秋浦歌

〔唐〕李白

白发三千丈，
缘愁似个长。
不知明镜里，
何处得秋霜。

14. *A Song in Qiupu*

〔Tang Dynasty〕By Li Bai

My gray hair grows three miles long,
As my worry becomes constant strong.
Looking into the mirror at my hair,
I wonder it is frost from somewhere.

译后小记

此诗是唐代伟大诗人李白的组诗作品《秋浦歌十七首》中的第十五首。这首诗大约作于唐玄宗李隆基时期的天宝末年，这时候唐王朝政治腐败，诗人对整个局势深感忧虑。此时，李白已经五十多岁了，理想不能实现，反而受到压抑和排挤。这怎不使诗人愁生白发，鬓染秋霜呢？

首句"白发三千丈"作了奇妙的夸张，七尺身躯何来三千丈的头发，根本不可能。读到下句"缘愁似个长"才豁然明白，因为愁思像这样长。"缘"，因为；"个长"，这么长。白发因愁而生，因愁而长。这三千丈的白发，是内心愁绪的象征。诗中有形的白发被无形的愁绪所替换，于是这三千丈的白发很自然地被理解为艺术的夸张。"三千丈"是虚数，不必字字对应，笔者翻译为 three miles long；而英语中的愁绪，用了 strong 来加强。

后两句"不知明镜里，何处得秋霜"是说：照着清亮的铜镜，看到自己的白发(Looking into the mirror at my hair)，简直没法知道自己的头发怎么会变得这样的白(I wonder it is frost from somewhere)，进一步加强对"愁"字的刻画，抒写了诗人愁肠百结难以自解的苦衷。"秋霜"代指白发，具有忧伤憔悴的感情色彩。

译诗行尾联韵 aabb。

15. 绝句

〔唐〕杜甫

两个黄鹂鸣翠柳，
一行白鹭上青天。
窗含西岭千秋雪，
门泊东吴万里船。

15. *A Quatrain*

〔Tang Dynasty〕By Du Fu

Two yellow orioles sing in the green willows;
A flock of white egrets fly into the blue sky
The snowed mountain is framed in windows;
By my gate the boat from Soochow does lie.

译后小记

此诗是唐代大诗人杜甫的组诗《绝句四首》的第三首。描写早春景象，四句四景。诗一开始表现出草堂的春色，诗人的情绪是陶然的，而随着视线的游移、景物的转换，江船的出现，便触动了他的乡情。全诗对仗精工，着色鲜丽，动静结合，声形兼俱，四句诗宛然组成一幅咫尺万里的壮阔山水画卷。

翻译此诗时,尽量对仗,前两句采用主动语句,第三句采用被动表达。用"苏州"(Soochow)来译"东吴",是部分代整体的认知转喻。

译诗隔行押韵 abab。

16. 春夜喜雨

〔唐〕杜甫

好雨知时节,
当春乃发生。
随风潜入夜,
润物细无声。
野径云俱黑,
江船火独明。
晓看红湿处,
花重锦官城。

16. *Timely Rain on a Spring Night*

〔Tang Dynasty〕By Du Fu

Good rain knows the proper time;
It arrives at the moment of spring.
Along with breeze it sneaks in night,
Quietly nourishing every little thing.
Dark clouds overspread the wild;
A boat on river looms solo light.
Dawn sees the saturated red mild;
The flowers adorn the city bright.

译后小记

《春夜喜雨》是唐代诗人杜甫创作的一首诗。此诗以极大的喜悦之情细致地描绘了春雨的特点和成都夜雨的景象,热情地讴歌了来得及时、滋润万物的春雨。诗人运用拟人手法,对春雨的描写,体悟精微,细腻生动,绘声绘形。全诗意境淡雅,意蕴清幽,诗境与画境浑然一体,是一首传神入化、别具风韵的咏雨诗。

诗题"春夜喜雨",笔者理解为及时雨,译为 Timely Rain on a Spring Night。翻译该诗,为再现拟人化手法的运用,注意动词的选择,如 knows, arrives, sneaks 等;语义表达贴近原义,语句自然流畅的同时,再追求一定的音韵效果。

翻译不必字字对应,且举一例"野径云俱黑"译为 Dark clouds overspread the wild,"野径"译为 the wild(荒野),不必照译 wild lane;"晓看红湿处",似乎有一处未曾明示,那就是雨后的鲜花更加柔媚,故笔者加一词 mild 作补语,刚好与 wild 形成对照,并押韵。

译诗尽量保留原诗意境,译诗译味,行尾押韵 ababcaca,第一行为元音韵,其他为完全韵。

17. 九月九日忆山东兄弟

〔唐〕王维

独在异乡为异客，
每逢佳节倍思亲。
遥知兄弟登高处，
遍插茱萸少一人。

17. Missing My Brothers on Double Ninth Festival

〔Tang Dynasty〕By Wang Wei

Alone, a lonely stranger in a land far away,
I miss my kinfolks deepest on festive day.
My brothers must be ascending a height,
All wearing dogberry without me in sight.

译后小记

《九月九日忆山东兄弟》是唐代诗人王维的名篇之一。此诗写出了游子的思乡怀亲之情。诗一开头便紧贴题目，写异乡异土生活的孤独凄然，因而时时怀乡思人，遇到佳节良辰，思念倍加。接着诗一跃而写远在家乡的兄弟，按照重阳节的风俗而登高时，也在怀念自己。诗意反复跳跃，含蓄深沉，既朴素自然，又曲折有致。其中"每逢佳节倍思亲"更是千古名句。

"九月九日"交代时间是重阳节,重阳登高是节日的一部分,故笔者译为 Double Ninth Festival。

"独在异乡为异客",开篇一句写出了诗人在异乡的孤独之感。诗人在这短短的一句话中用了一个"独"、两个"异"字,笔者翻译时化为三个短语 alone, a lonely stranger, in a land far away;"每逢佳节倍思亲"中的"倍"是程度,并非倍数,笔者用了最高级"deepest"来表示。

"遥知兄弟登高处,遍插茱萸少一人",诗人遥想兄弟们在重阳佳节登上高山,身上插着茱萸,可惜只少我一人(My brothers must be ascending a height, All wearing dogberry without me in sight)。

译诗行尾联韵 aabb。

18. 山居秋暝

〔唐〕王维

空山新雨后，
天气晚来秋。
明月松间照，
清泉石上流。
竹喧归浣女，
莲动下渔舟。
随意春芳歇，
王孙自可留。

18. *Autumn Dusk in Mountains*

〔Tang Dynasty〕By Wang Wei

A shower washes open mountains clear;
Autumn permeates the cool evening air.
Through pine-trees the moonlight peers;
O'er mossy stones the clear spring cheers.
Bamboo bustle tells the wash-girls near;
Swaying lotus knows fishing boats here.
Though the spring fragrance fades away,
In autumn here is a place you may stay.

译后小记

《山居秋暝》描绘了秋雨初晴后傍晚时分山村的旖旎风光和山居村民的淳朴风尚，表现了诗人寄情山水田园并对隐居生活怡然自得的满足心情，以自然美来表现人格美和社会美。全诗将空山雨后的秋凉，松间明月的光照，石上清泉的声音以及浣女归来竹林中的喧笑声，渔船穿过荷花的动态，和谐完美地融合在一起，给人一种丰富新鲜的感受。它像一幅清新秀丽的山水画，又像一支恬静优美的抒情乐曲，体现了王维诗中有画的创作特点。

首联是写雨后山中秋景，"空山"乃空旷，空寂的山野（open mountains），刚刚下过一场雨，山野洗刷得透亮，傍晚的空气渗透着秋意。

颔联天色已暝，却有皓月当空，青松如盖；山泉清冽，淙淙流泻于山石之上。翻译采用了拟人手法，用到了 peer 和 cheer，同时兼顾对仗。

颈联中诗人先写"竹喧"再写"莲动"，因为浣女隐在竹林之中，渔舟被莲叶遮蔽，起初未见，等到听到竹林喧声，看到莲叶纷披，才发现浣女、莲舟。这样写更富有真情实感，更富有诗意。原诗为倒装句，笔者翻译时用了动词 tell 和 know，一对类似句子结构。

尾联则是诗人有感而发。虽然春光已逝，但秋景更佳，愿意留下来，翻译时加连词 though。

19. 画

〔唐〕王维

远看山有色,
近听水无声。
春去花还在,
人来鸟不惊。

19. *A Painting*

〔Tang Dynasty〕By Wang Wei

Seen from afar, the hills are in hue;
Heard nearby, the brooks are mute.
Spring is gone but flowers are abloom;
The birds remain no matter you shoo.

译后小记

此诗描写的是自然景物,赞叹的却是一幅画。前两句写其山色分明,流水无声;后两句描述其花开四季,鸟不怕人。四句诗构成了一幅完整的山水花鸟图。全诗对仗工整,尤其是诗中多组反义词的运用,使其节奏清晰,平仄分明,韵味十足,读着朗朗上口。

"远看山有色,近听水无声"的翻译(Seen from afar, the hills are in

hue; Heard nearby, the brooks are mute.）亦基本对仗。"春去花还在，人来鸟不惊"，两个小句都是转折关系，故用 but 而不用 and。译诗行尾押东方韵 aaba。

20. 送元二使安西

〔唐〕王维

渭城朝雨浥轻尘,
客舍青青柳色新。
劝君更进一杯酒,
西出阳关无故人。

20. *A Farewell Song*

〔Tang Dynasty〕By Wang Wei

No dust is raised after the morning rain;
The willows near the hotel are fresh green.
Come on, buddy, have another glass of wine;
Getting out of Pass Yangguan, I'm not thine.

译后小记

　　送元二使安西(一作渭城曲),描写的是一种朋友间的离别,故译为 A Farewell Song。前两句写渭城驿馆风景,送别的时间、地点、环境气氛,构成了一幅色调清新明朗的图景。后二句转入伤别,却不着伤字,只用举杯劝酒来表达内心强烈深沉的离别之情。

　　长期以来,"西出阳关"一直被简单理解为友人走出了阳关,但是在这里却是"一语双关":它按照时空的发展次序有着两幅截然不同的场景,第一幅"西出阳关"是指友人在征途中刚刚走出了阳关,渭城在东,阳关在西,是谓"西面出去",一般人们均持此种观点;另一幅"西出阳关"就是指友人在经历千辛万苦,完成了任务凯旋而归时离开了阳关,渭城仍在东,阳关仍在西,却是谓"西面出来"。

诗人这两句其实是运用了逆挽(即叙事题材的"倒叙")并结合了省略的写作手法,引导读者的思绪跟随年轻的友人一起奔赴疆域,然后历经万种艰险,最后凯旋而归时,而"我"——现在的这个送行者却恐怕因年老多病已不在人世了,这一情景更添离愁伤感。历史的真实是,诗人在送走友人后不满六年(于761年)便与世长辞了。

"劝君更进一杯酒,西出阳关无故人",译者采用直接跟友人对话的口吻,"西出阳关"保留原文的双关之意,译为 Getting out of Pass Yangguan,留待译文读者自己去解读。

21. 鹿柴

〔唐〕王维

空山不见人，
但闻人语响。
返景入深林，
复照青苔上。

21. *The Deer Enclosure*

〔Tang Dynasty〕By Wang Wei

The mountain sees no man in sight,
But simply echoes some human voices.
In the deep forest peeps no sunlight,
But some sunbeams Leaking on mosses.

译后小记

第一句"空山不见人"，先正面描写空山的杳无人迹。王维特别喜欢用"空山"这个词语，在不同的诗里表现不同境界。此诗中，由于杳无人迹，这并不真空的山在诗人的感觉中显得空廓虚无，宛如太古之境。"不见人"，把"空山"的意蕴具体化了。第二句"但闻人语响"，却境界顿出。"但闻"二字颇可玩味。翻译时两句都以 the mountain 作主语，采用拟人化手法译出，这里的"闻"理解为"回响"。

第三、第四句"返景入深林，复照青苔上"，由上幅的描写空山中人语进而描写深林返照，由声而色。深林幽暗，林间树下的青苔，更突出了深林的不见阳光。一抹余晖射入幽暗的深林，斑斑驳驳的树影照映在树下的青苔上时，那一小片光影和大片的无边的幽暗所构成的强烈对比，反而使深林的幽暗更加突出。这里"照"在青苔上的阳光，是密林漏下的光点。

　　翻译此诗时，笔者设法表达出原诗中"以人语反衬幽静""以青苔上的光点反衬幽暗"的意境。注意选词，如 echo、leak。译诗行尾押交韵 abab，并有行中头韵，行中腹韵。

22. 相思

〔唐〕王维

红豆生南国,
春来发几枝。
愿君多采撷,
此物最相思。

22. *Love Seeds*

〔Tang Dynasty〕By Wang Wei

Red beans grow in the southern land;
Spring sees twigs sprout one by one.
May you pluck them with each hand,
For they are symbols of deepest love.

译后小记

《相思》是王维创作的一首借咏物而寄相思的五绝。此诗写相思之情,首句写红豆产地;次句以"发几枝"极富形象性;三句寄意友人"多采撷",言在此而意在彼;末句点明其相思属性,且用"最"字推达极致,则"多采撷"的理由自见,而自身所寄之意亦深含其中。全诗极为明快,却又委婉含蓄,语浅而情深。

相思子,别称红豆,藤本,茎细弱,多分枝,广泛分布于热带地区。荚果长圆形,果瓣革质,成熟时开裂,有种子2~6粒;种子椭圆形,平滑具光泽,上部约三分之二为鲜红色,下部三分之一为黑色。种子可以做成珠串饰物与打击乐器。由此可见,红豆可译为 red beans 或 red seeds;结合诗中寓意,诗题可译为 Love Seeds,不但可指实物的红豆,还可喻指爱的种子。

第二句"春来发几枝",笔者认为不是问句,而是描述其春天长枝叶;第三句"愿君多采撷",笔者用 May sb. do sth. 表示希望,不用简单的祈使句;"此物最相思"交代原因,笔者用了 for,此物承载最深的相思(For they are symbols of deepest love)。

23. 黄鹤楼

〔唐〕崔颢

昔人已乘黄鹤去,
此地空余黄鹤楼。
黄鹤一去不复返,
白云千载空悠悠。
晴川历历汉阳树,
芳草萋萋鹦鹉洲。
日暮乡关何处是?
烟波江上使人愁。

23. *Yellow Crane Tower*

〔Tang Dynasty〕By Cui Hao

The sage on yellow crane has flown away;
Alone the empty Tower here does stay.
The bygone crane will never be back again,
With clouds afloat thro' year by year in vain.
The sunlit trees by river are clearly seen;
Wild grass on Parrot Islet are lush green.
Where my hometown lies in faint twilight?
The misty river takes on a gloomy sight.

译后小记

崔颢《黄鹤楼》一诗有风骨、有兴象、有情思,是歌行与七律完美结合的佳作。格律诗在初唐虽已成熟定型,实则古体诗与格律诗同时流行,尚未完全摆脱古风格调。《黄鹤楼》一诗亦古亦律,吊古怀今,以诗言志,一气呵成,气势磅礴,浑然天成。从崔颢《黄鹤楼》看出"形"可以因"气韵"而破格,在诗歌翻译时,我们也追求"形神兼备",但"神似"更重要。

原诗隔行押韵,一韵到底;译诗主旋律为五音步抑扬格,行尾押联韵 aabbccdd。

译诗格律分析如下:

> The sage on yellow crane has flown away;
> Alone the empty Tower here does stay.
> The bygone crane will never be back again,
> With clouds afloat thro' year by year in vain.
> The sunlit trees by river are clearly seen;
> Wild grass on Parrot Islet are lush green.
> Where my hometown lies in faint twilight?
> The misty river takes on gloomy sight.

24. 忆江南

〔唐〕白居易

江南好，
风景旧曾谙。
日出江花红胜火，
春来江水绿如蓝。
能不忆江南？

24. *A Wisp of Memory of the Southern Shore*

〔Tang Dynasty〕By Bai Juyi

Southern shore was fine
With scenes impressed on my mind.
At sunrise the flowers at the riverside seemed afire;
In spring river water was blue as sapphire.
How can I not admire?

译后小记

《忆江南》为白居易晚年所作，为追忆青年时期，漫游江南，旅居苏杭所感受到的江南盛景。仅用几十个字江南美景便跃然眼前，令人心驰神往。

诗题"忆江南"的"忆"第一次译为 Dreaming of…,不是追忆,第二次改为名词 memories,第三次改为 a wisp of memory,总算满意。"江南",是指地理区域,顾名思义,意为"长江之南",并不好译,暂且译为 the Southern Shore。

诗词的翻译,为了画面呈现和直观体验,笔者少用过去时态,但这一次的"忆"采用了过去时态。译文分为三句话,首先说"江南给我留下深刻印象"(Southern shore was fine / With scenes impressed on my mind.),然后具体讲江南之美"日出江花红胜火,春来江水绿如蓝"(At sunrise the flowers at the riverside seemed afire; In spring river water was blue as sapphire)。最后,强调"能不忆江南?(How can I not admire?)

译文有一定音韵效果,行尾押韵 aabbb。

25. 草

〔唐〕白居易

离离原上草，
一岁一枯荣。
野火烧不尽，
春风吹又生。
远芳侵古道，
晴翠接荒城。
又送王孙去，
萋萋满别情。

25. Grass on the Ancient Plain

〔Tang Dynasty〕By Bai Zhuyi

Lush grass overruns the ancient plain;
Once in a year they bloom and fade.
Prairie fire tries to burn them in vain;
Spring breezes blow them green again.
Fragrant grass invades the ancient road,
Verdure view to the desert town though.
My friend bids farewell here and apart;
Flourishing grass knows my broken heart.

译后小记

《草》是唐代诗人白居易的成名作。"野火烧不尽,春风吹又生。"赞扬野草的顽强生命力,野草的韧劲和不服输。

那一片原野上的野草是如此的茂盛,秋来枯萎,春来翠绿。即便是无情的大火也烧不完这无尽的野草,来年春风吹过,它们又将铺满原野。它们一片片向远处蔓延,淹没了荒城与古道,晴空之下,显得越发的青翠。在这原野之上,我又一次的送别我的朋友,这原野上的每一根草的每片叶子,都满载着我的深情。

"离离""萋萋"都是青草茂盛的样子,译诗用了两个不同的词 lush 和 flushing 表达。翻译此诗,在传达诗意的同时,注意音韵节奏。

26. 借问江潮与海水

〔唐〕白居易

借问江潮与海水，
何似君情与妾心？
相恨不如潮有信，
相思始觉海非深。

26. *May I Ask Sea Water and River Tides*

〔Tang Dynasty〕By Bai Juyi

May I ask sea water and river tides;
Are you just like man and his wife?
Tides are more trustworthy sometimes;
The sea isn't deep as my lovesick mind.

译后小记

《借问江潮与海水》是唐代诗人白居易创作的一首词，这首词形式与七言绝句相同。该词通过自问自答的形式来写闺情，真实地表现出她对爱情的忠贞和被人抛弃的悲惨境遇。

首二句"借问江潮与海水，何似君情与妾心"发问，以水喻情。"江潮"常汹涌而来，倏忽而去，与薄幸人起初热烈却又转瞬即逝的爱情极为相似。大海既深且广，有如思妇对情人的思念。但词中思妇却认为江和海水不能与自己的情意相比。"相恨不如潮有信,相思始觉海非深",上二句设问,这两句予以回答。"江潮"纵然倏忽而逝,但它日日夜夜有来有往,而那负心郎呢?他走后却再没有音信。海水纵然很深,却不及自己对"君"的情意深厚。

"君情与妾心"正好借用《圣经》中的 man and his wife 来译,在理解原文的基础上,表达出诗意,译诗有一定音韵效果。行尾押元音韵 aaaa。

27. 苦热题恒寂师禅室

〔唐〕白居易

人人避暑走如狂,
独有禅师不出房;
可是禅房无热到?
但能心静身即凉。

27. A Poem to Zen Master Hengji Written on His Meditation Wall in Dog Days

〔Tang Dynasty〕By Bai Juyi

Hustle and bustle, people flee from heat;
Cool and calm, Master mediates in seat.
Is the meditation abode cool in dog days?
But a peaceful mind feels refreshed always.

译后小记

诗中"人人",非英语之 everyone,以 people 译之。后两句,可理解为有问号的"可是禅房无热到?"。诗人以修辞性的反意疑问句自问自答:"但能心静即身凉!"这样,诗意更浓,意境更奇。

夏日炎炎,禅室也不例外;但出家人无纷繁的干扰,心闲静则觉凉。"心静身凉"乃禅意深厚,蕴含哲理。译文采用尾韵 hustle and bustle 来描写众人的熙攘忙乱，头韵 cool and calm 来突出禅师的心境平和，一静一动形成对比，与原文诗意一致。原诗中"苦热""避暑"等词，可知当时必定是"酷暑""三伏天"一类，故采用 dog days 译之。译诗多处采用头韵、尾韵，全诗韵式为 aabb，力争再现原文意境和诗意。

28. 重阳席上赋白菊

〔唐〕白居易

满园花菊郁金黄,
中有孤丛色似霜。
还似今朝歌酒席,
白头翁入少年场。

28. Ode to the White Chrysanthemums on Double Ninth Festival

〔Tang Dynasty〕By Bai Juyi

Among thousands of chrysanthemums gold,
A cluster of mums white as frost I behold,
Like a grey-headed in the youngsters' revelry,
Drinking, dancing and playing, so merry!

译后小记

《重阳席上赋白菊》是唐代诗人白居易创作的一首七言绝句。此诗前两句写诗人看到满园金黄的菊花中有一朵雪白的菊花,感到欣喜;后两句把那朵雪白的菊花比作是参加"歌舞席"的老人,和"少年"一起载歌载舞。全诗表达了诗人虽然年老仍有少年的情趣。以花喻人,饶有情趣。

"还似今朝歌酒席,白头翁入少年场",翻译时省去了"今朝",在诗歌语境中,此意自明;加上了"Drinking, dancing and playing, so merry!"将"白头翁入少年场"的欢快情景具体化了。

全诗正常语序为:Among thousands of gold chrysanthemums, I behold a cluster of mums white as frost, like a grey-headed in the youngsters' revelry, drinking, dancing and playing, so merry。

译诗行尾押韵 aabb。

29. 惜牡丹花

〔唐〕白居易

惆怅阶前红牡丹,
晚来唯有两枝残。
明朝风起应吹尽,
夜惜衰红把火看。

29. *Poor Peony*

〔Tang Dynasty〕By Bai Juyi

Disconsolate I see the peonies by the doorway;
Toward evening, two flowers are left but fade.
The wind might blast them next day I'm afraid;
I'd take a long, long look by lantern right away.

译后小记

诗人在牡丹盛开之时,就想到其红衰之日,并以"把火看"表现了怜惜之情,寄寓了青春难驻的感慨,而发出要把握时机、珍惜一切美好事物的感慨!

诗题"惜牡丹花",翻译时省略了动词"惜",译为 Poor Peony,怜惜之情蕴含其中。

译诗时体验诗人的情感,关注语义、情感、音韵节奏的表达和体现。译诗行尾押抱韵 abba。

30. 池上

〔唐〕白居易

小娃撑小艇，
偷采白莲回。
不解藏踪迹，
浮萍一道开。

30. *On the Pool*

〔Tang Dynasty〕By Bai Juyi

A little kid poles a little boat
Back slyly from stealing lotus.
He knows not to hide his trace
With the duckweeds apart afloat.

译后小记

《池上》是唐代诗人白居易创作的五言绝句，此诗写一个小孩儿偷采白莲的情景，也是自己心态的一种反映。诗人以其通俗风格，将两个小景写得可爱、可亲、可信，富有韵味。

首句"小娃撑小艇"的"撑"，可用 pole，也可用 punt，但 pole 与 boat 押腹韵；翻译"偷采白莲回"时，笔者加了 slyly 一词，似乎将小娃"偷偷地"样子更加会意地呈现；译诗有一定音韵节奏，不乏童趣。

31. 大林寺桃花

〔唐〕白居易

人间四月芳菲尽,
山寺桃花始盛开。
长恨春归无觅处,
不知转入此中来。

31. Peach Blossoms in the Temple of Great Forest

〔Tang Dynasty〕By Bai Juyi

In Lunar April flowers fade in flat ground;
Peach blossoms just bloom on the hillside.
I oft regret for spring nowhere to be found;
Oh, she turns out to come here and hide.

译后小记

《大林寺桃花》是诗人于元和十二年(817年)初夏在江州(今九江)庐山上大林寺时即景吟成的一首七绝。此诗说初夏四月作者来到大林寺,此时山下芳菲已尽,而不期在山寺中遇上了一片刚刚盛开的桃花。诗中写出了作者触目所见的感受,突出地展示了发现的惊讶与意外的欣喜。

"人间四月芳菲尽,山寺桃花始盛开",诗中第一句的"芳菲尽",与第二句的"始盛开",是在对比中遥相呼应的,仿佛从人间的现实世界,突然步入一个仙境,置身于非人间的另一世界。正是在这一感受的触发下,诗人想象的翅膀飞腾起来了。"长恨春归无觅处,不知转入此中来。"诗人想到,自己曾因为惜春、恋春,以至怨恨春去的无情,但谁知却是错怪了春,原来春并未归去,只不过像小孩子跟人捉迷藏一样,偷偷地躲到这块地方罢了。

古时都是阴历,"人间四月"译为 Lunar April;翻译此诗,体验诗人的感受,运用拟人手法,如 hide;译诗行尾押交韵 abab,行中有头韵,如第一行 flower、fade、flat,第二行 blossom、bloom,第三行 for、fond,第四行 here、hide 等。

译诗行尾押交韵 abab。

32. 暮江吟

〔唐〕白居易

一道残阳铺水中,
半江瑟瑟半江红。
可怜九月初三夜,
露似真珠月似弓。

32. *Chant to Twilight River*

〔Tang Dynasty〕By Bai Juyi

A slant of sunbeams is paved in the river;
Half is tinted rose and the other half shiver.
On the third of lunar September, what a view!
The dews are pearls, the crescent a bow.

译后小记

《暮江吟》是唐代诗人白居易创作的一首七绝。这是一首写景佳作。诗人选取了红日西沉到新月东升这一段时间里的两组景物进行描写,运用了新颖巧妙的比喻,创造出和谐、宁静的意境,通过吟咏表现出内心深处的情思和对大自然的热爱之情。

前两句写夕阳落照中的江水。"一道残阳铺水中",残阳照射在江面上,不说"照",却说"铺",这是因为"残阳"已经接近地平线,几乎是贴着地面照射过来，确像"铺"在江上，很形象；译诗也用 pave，不用 burst through 或 thrust through，shine 等。"半江瑟瑟半江红"，江水缓缓流动，江面皱起细小的波纹，受光多的部分，呈现一片"红"色；受光少的地方，呈现出深深的碧色。"瑟瑟"又让人联想起"瑟瑟发抖"，原来用的 blue 又被换作 shiver；水中残阳的"红"，译者选择了 rose；"可怜九月初三夜，露似真珠月似弓"，诗人通过对"露""月"的视觉形象描写，创造出和谐、宁静的意境，用这样新颖巧妙的比喻来精心为大自然敷彩着色，描容绘形，给读者展现了一幅绝妙的画卷。"可怜"是作者脱口赞美它的可爱，不可译为 poor。

译诗力求传达原诗中日落前后江景之美，有一定音韵效果。

33. 咏鹅

〔唐〕骆宾王

鹅，鹅，鹅，
曲项向天歌。
白毛浮绿水，
红掌拨清波。

33. *Ode to Goose*

〔Tang Dynasty〕By Luo Bingwang

Goose, goose, goose,
Neck bent, head raised, singing.
White plumes on green water, floating,
Red palms in clear ripples, paddling.

译后小记

《咏鹅》是初唐诗人骆宾王于七岁时写的一首五言古诗。这首诗开篇先声夺人，"鹅！鹅！鹅！"写出鹅的声响美，又通过"曲项"与"向天"、"白毛"与"绿水"、"红掌"与"清波"的对比写出鹅的线条美与色彩美，同时，"歌""浮""拨"等字又写出鹅的动态美，听觉与视觉、静态与动态、音声与色彩完美结合，将鹅的形神活现而出。

汉语的"鹅"，英语的goose，都是以叫声来命名，翻译时，第一行对应而译，轻易得来；第二句分为"曲项""向天""歌"三个语义来表达。三、四句，诗人用一组对偶句，着重从色彩方面来铺叙鹅群戏水的情况。鹅的毛是白的，而江水却是绿的，"白""绿"对照，鲜明耀眼，这是当句对；同样，鹅掌是红的，而水波是青的，"红""青"映衬，十分艳丽，这也是当句对。翻译时也注意句式对仗和颜色对比，力求画面生动。

34. 咏柳

〔唐〕贺知章

碧玉妆成一树高，
万条垂下绿丝绦。
不知细叶谁裁出？
二月春风似剪刀。

34. *Ode to the Willow*

〔Tang Dynasty〕By He Zhizhang

The tree is dressed in green jade so fair,
Myriads of green fringes drooping there.
I wonder who has cut out the fine leaves?
Oh, the tailor is the early spring breeze.

译后小记

《咏柳》是盛唐诗人贺知章写的一首七言绝句。这首诗是一首咏物诗。诗的前两句连用两个唯美的意象，描绘春柳的勃勃生气，葱翠袅娜；后两句更别出心裁地把春风比喻为"剪刀"，将视之无形不可捉摸的"春风"形象地表现出来，不仅立意新奇，而且饱含诗韵。

前两句描绘春柳，译文(The tree is dressed in green jade so fair;

Myriads of green fringes drooping there.）将婀娜春柳呈现读者眼前；后面句，一问，（I wonder who has cut out the fine leaves? Oh, the tailor is the early spring breeze.）将春风拟人译出。译诗行尾押联韵 aabb。

35. 回乡偶书

〔唐〕贺知章

少小离家老大回，
乡音无改鬓毛衰。
儿童相见不相识，
笑问客从何处来。

35. A Whim About Home-Coming

〔Tang Dynasty〕By He Zhizhang

I come back home that I left young
With grey hair and a native tongue.
The kids don't know me when we meet;
"Where are you from? Sir!" they greet.

译后小记

此诗写于作者晚年辞官还乡之时，抒发作者久客他乡的伤感的同时，也写出了久别回乡的亲切感。

"偶书"，即随便写的诗。"偶"，指诗写作得很偶然，是随时有所见、有所感就写下来的。笔者想到一词 whim。

前两句在译诗中化为一个完整句子(I come back home that I left young with grey hair and a native tongue)；"儿童相见不相识"，这里的

儿童大概不应该是自己的孩子吧，大概是家乡的孩童看见我，没有一个认识我，故译为 The kids I meet cannot recognize me；"笑问客从何处来"，译诗以直接引语来表达，以求亲切自然。

译诗但求流畅自然，有一定音韵节奏，行尾押联韵 aabb。

36. 登幽州台歌

〔唐〕陈子昂

前不见古人,
后不见来者。
念天地之悠悠,
独怆然而涕下!

36. *On the Tower of Youzhou*

〔Tang Dynasty〕By Chen Zi'ang

I see no greats of the past,
Neither any greats follow.
The sky and earth are vast;
Alone, I shed tears of sorrow.

译后小记

《登幽州台歌》这首短诗,没有对幽州台作一字描写,而只是登台的感慨,却成为千古名篇,深刻地表现了诗人怀才不遇、寂寞无聊的情绪。

前二句俯仰古今,写出了时间的漫长;这里的"古人"是指古代那些能够礼贤下士的贤明君主,译文用 greats(伟人)来译。第三句登楼眺望,写出了空间的辽阔;第四句描绘了诗人孤独寂寞苦闷的情绪,两相映照，分外动人，读来酣畅淋漓又余音缭绕。

译诗保持一定节奏和韵律，行尾押交韵 abab，节奏分析如下：

I see/ no greats /of the past,

Nither/ any greats /follow.

The sky/ and earth/ are vast;

Alone, / I shed tears/ of sorrow.

37. 题都城南庄

〔唐〕崔护

去年今日此门中，
人面桃花相映红。
人面不知何处去，
桃花依旧笑春风。

37. Written in a Village Southern of the Capital

〔Tang Dynasty〕By Cui Hu

Inside the gate, this time last year,
Pink face outshone peach flowers here.
I find the face today nowhere,
But flowers smile in air o'er there.

译后小记

这首诗设置了两个场景，"寻春遇艳"与"重寻不遇"，虽然场景相同，却是物是人非。

诗的开头两句是追忆。"去年今日此门中"，点出时间和地点，写得非常具体，足见这个时间和地点，在诗人心中留下了多么深刻难忘的记忆。第二句是写人，"人面"竟能"映"得桃花分外红艳，则"人面"

之美可以想见。面对着这一幅色彩浓丽、青春焕发、两美相辉的人面桃花图,不用说姑娘的神采美貌如在目前,就是她的情态,诗人的心事,彼此藏在心中的欢爱和兴奋,也都是可以"思而得之"的。

后两句,人面杳然,依旧含笑的桃花只能引动对往事的美好回忆和好景不常在的感慨了。"依旧"二字,正含有无限怅惘。

翻译此诗,推敲过两个字,"门"是 gate 还是 door;"映"应如何表达。译诗采用四音步抑扬格,节奏与原诗同,行尾押韵 aabb。

38. 江雪

〔唐〕柳宗元

千山鸟飞绝,
万径人踪灭。
孤舟蓑笠翁,
独钓寒江雪。

38. *Fishing Snow*

〔Tang Dynasty〕By Liu Zongyuan

Hills upon hills no bird in flight,
Path to path no footprints in sight.
A lone fishman in his coir raincoat
Is fishing snow alone in his boat.

译后小记

《江雪》是唐代诗人柳宗元于永州创作的一首五言绝句。诗中运用典型概括的手法,选择千山万径,人鸟绝迹这种最能表现山野严寒的典型景物,描绘大雪纷飞,天寒地冻的图景;接着勾画独钓寒江的渔翁形象,借以表达诗人在遭受打击之后不屈而又深感孤寂的情绪。这首诗藏着四个字"千万孤独"。

笔者用 hills upon hills 来译"千山",path to path 来译"万径";"鸟

飞绝"译为 no bird in flight,"人踪灭"译为 no footprints in sight。前两句译文如原诗对仗,后两行实则一句话,即 A lone fishman in his coir raincoat /Is fishing snow alone in his boat。

译诗行尾押联韵 aabb,诗中多腹韵/ əʊ/。

39. 清明

〔唐〕杜牧

清明时节雨纷纷,
路上行人欲断魂。
借问酒家何处有,
牧童遥指杏花村。

39. *Qingming Festival*

〔Tang Dynasty〕By Du Mu

It drizzles thick on the Mourning Day;
The pedestrian feels sad on the way.
"Where can I find a tavern, cowboy?"
He points to the Apricot Village faraway.

译后小记

清明节,又称踏青节、行清节、三月节、祭祖节等,英文有 Tomb-sweeping Day, Qingming Festival, Pure Brightness Festival。此诗写清明春雨中所见,诗题还是选择了 Qingming Festival。诗中的"清明时节"根据下文"路上行人欲断魂",选择了 the Mourning Day,希望读者能在语篇中建立联系。

第三句,到底是谁在问"借问酒家何处有",不同学者有不同解释,笔者将其转换为直接问句"Where can I find a tavern, cowboy?"读者可根据自己的理解去解读。"杏花村"是回答"何处",故笔者将其理解为一个村子的名称。

译诗押东方韵 aaba。

40. 山行

〔唐〕杜牧

远上寒山石径斜,
白云生处有人家。
停车坐爱枫林晚,
霜叶红于二月花。

40. *A Mountain Trip*

〔Tang Dynasty〕By Du Mu

To the mount afar a stony path is slanting;
A cottage gleams in the puffy clouds flowing.
I pull up my cart at the maple woods gazing;
Frost-blasted leaves outshine flowers in spring.

译后小记

此诗描绘秋日山行所见的景色,展现出一幅动人的山林秋色图,山路、人家、白云、红叶,构成一幅和谐统一的画面,表现了作者的高怀逸兴和豪荡思致。

"远上寒山石径斜"(To the mount afar a stony path is slanting),写山,写山路。一条弯弯曲曲的小路蜿蜒伸向山头。"远"字写出了山路的绵长,"斜"字与"上"字呼应,写出了高而缓的山势,以 slanting 译

"斜"。

"白云生处有人家"（A cottage gleams in the puffy clouds flowing），写云，写人家。诗人的目光顺着这条山路一直向上望去，在白云飘浮的地方，有处农家宅院，以 flowing 译"生"。

"停车坐爱枫林晚"（I pull up my cart at the maple woods gazing），诗人的倾向性已经很鲜明，很强烈了。那山路、白云、人家都没有使诗人动心，这枫林晚景却使得他惊喜之情难以抑制，这里的 gazing 出于语境需要。

"霜叶红于二月花"（Frost-blasted leaves outshine flowers in spring）补足第三句，一片深秋枫林美景具体呈现出来了，主要是为了突显霜叶的美。译诗在这里将"二月花"简单处理为 flowers in spring。

译者并不追求 -ing 结尾的单词来押韵，行尾的四个单词全是出于自然语义表达需要。

41. 望洞庭

〔唐〕刘禹锡

湖光秋月两相和,
潭面无风镜未磨。
遥望洞庭山水翠,
白银盘里一青螺。

41. *Lake Dongting Viewed Afar*

〔Tang Dynasty〕By Liu Yuxi

The autumn moon merges into the lake;
An unpolished mirror is the surface still.
Seen afar, in the clear water a verdant hill
Looks like a green field snail on a silver plate.

译后小记

此诗描写了秋夜月光下洞庭湖的优美景色,表达了诗人对洞庭风光的喜爱和赞美之情。全诗选择了月夜遥望的角度,把千里洞庭尽收眼底,抓住最有代表性的湖光山色,轻轻着笔,通过丰富的想象、巧妙的比喻,独出心裁地把洞庭美景再现于纸上,显示出惊人的艺术功力。

首句(The autumn moon merges into the lake)描写湖水与素月交相

辉映的景象，第二句描绘无风时湖面平静的情状，译诗换了个角度将此句译出（An unpolished mirror is the surface still）；第三、第四句集中描写湖中的君山（Seen afar, in the clear water a verdant hill / Looks like a green field snail on a silver plate），译诗用了一个跨行诗句。

译诗行尾押抱韵 abba。

42. 秋词

〔唐〕刘禹锡

自古逢秋悲寂寥，
我言秋日胜春朝。
晴空一鹤排云上，
便引诗情到碧霄。

42. *Ode to Autumn*

〔Tang Dynasty〕By Liu Yuxi

From of old, autumn is a time for moan;
I'd say autumn days surpass spring morns.
A crane, soaring into lofty clouds on high,
Inspires my poetic spirit to the blue sky.

译后小记

《秋词二首》是唐代诗人刘禹锡的组诗作品之一。诗人对秋天和秋色的感受与众不同，一反过去文人悲秋的传统，赞颂了秋天的美好，并借黄鹤直冲云霄的描写，表现了作者奋发进取的豪情和豁达乐观的情怀。

"自古逢秋悲寂寥"（From of old, autumn is a time for moan），诗人开篇，即以议论起笔，断然否定了前人悲秋的观念，表现出一种激越向上的诗情。"秋日胜春朝"（autumn days surpass spring morns），用对比手法，热情赞美秋天，说秋天比那万物萌生，欣欣向荣的春天更胜过一筹，这是对自古以来那种悲秋的论调的有力否定。

"晴空一鹤排云上，便引诗情到碧霄"（A crane, soaring into lofty clouds on high, ／ Inspires my poetic spirit to the blue sky）展现的，不仅仅是秋天的生机和素色，更多的是一种高扬的气概和高尚的情操。

43. 八至

〔唐〕李冶

至近至远东西，
至深至浅清溪。
至高至明日月，
至亲至疏夫妻。

43. *Eight Extremes*

〔Tang Dynasty〕By Li Ye

The nearest but farthest: east and west;
The shallowest but deepest: a clear creek;
The highest but brightest: the sun and moon;
The closest but distant most: man and wife.

译后小记

《八至》是唐代女诗人李冶创作的六言诗。此诗首字"至"字在诗中反复出现八次，故题名"八至"。从内容上说，全诗四句，说的都是浅显而至真的道理，具有深刻的辩证法，富有哲理意味。从结构上说，作者设置了层云叠嶂，前三句只是个过场，主要是为了引出最后一句"至亲至疏夫妻"，专在针砭世情，极为冷峻。

这个诗题的翻译颇伤脑筋，英语的最高级有加-est 或 most 两种，

"八至"最后译为 Eight Extremes(八个极端)，表义接近，押头韵。

"至近至远东西"，"东西"说近就近，可以间隔为零，"至近"之谓也。如果东西向方向相反，甚至无穷远，仍不外乎一东一西，可见"东西"说远也远，乃至"至远"。这里的"至远"是物理空间，不宜译为 furthest。

"至深至浅清溪"，清溪不比江河湖海，一目了然能看到水底，"浅"是实情，是其所以为溪的特征之一。然而，它又有"深"的假象，特别是水流缓慢近于清池的溪流，可以倒映云鸟、涵泳星月，形成上下天光，令人莫测浅深，因此也可以说是深的。翻译时，不宜译为 The deepest but shallowest。

"至高至明日月"，理解这句应置身于诗人当时的年代去感受，日月同辉是人们的感觉，日月并举是向有的惯例，以此入诗，也无可挑剔。这里的"高"，断不可译为 tall；日月并举，所以共用一个冠词 the。

前三句虽属三个范畴，而它们偏于物理的辩证法，唯有末句专指人情言之，是全诗结穴所在——"至亲至疏夫妻"。如果说前三句还能以 and 连接几个"至"，这一句是绝不可能。夫妻本应是"至亲"，可现实成了"至疏"，这是诗人对于封建社会夫妻关系的感受。这里，笔者选择两个表达心理空间远近的词 close, distant，不宜用 far(一般指物理空间)来译

译诗中，冒号相当谓语动词 is；相反或相对的词为一对，故共用一个 the，如 The nearest but farthest；"至近至远""至深至浅""至高至明""至亲至疏"之间都是对比关系，故中间用连接词 but，而不用 and。(因为四个 but，笔者还有一个版本，将"八至"译为 Four Buts。)最后"夫妻"不是 husband and wife，而是 man and wife。

44. 一七令·茶

〔唐〕元稹

茶。

香叶，嫩芽。

慕诗客，爱僧家。

碾雕白玉，罗织红纱。

铫煎黄蕊色，碗转曲尘花。

夜后邀陪明月，晨前命对朝霞。

洗尽古今人不倦，将至醉后岂堪夸。

44. *Song of One to Seven Words · Tea*

〔Tang Dynasty〕Yuan Zhen

Tea

Leaves sweet, buds tender

Poets adore it, monks admire it

White jade the mill, red yarn the screen

Fry out soft yellow mellow, skim off the tea foam

A sip of tea in moonlight, a cup of tea in sunlight

One will wash away the daily weary, lift up the spirit and be merry

译后小记

一七令，在中国古代诗词中较为少见。元稹的这首词，先后表达了三层意思：一是从茶的本性说到了人们对茶的喜爱；二是从茶的煎煮说到了人们的饮茶习俗；三是就茶的功用说到了茶能提神醒酒。

此词不但形美，意美，还音美。

译文每行单词数与原词字数一样逐行递增，也构成一七令。语义贴近原诗，行内腹韵，如 leaves sweet；行内头韵，如 adore 与 admire；行内尾韵，如 yellow mellow, moonlight 与 sunlight, weary 与 merry 等；但美中不足的是行尾没能押韵。

45. 凉州词

〔唐〕王翰

葡萄美酒夜光杯，
欲饮琵琶马上催。
醉卧沙场君莫笑，
古来征战几人回？

45. *Liangzhou Song*

〔Tang Dynasty〕By Wang Han

The jade cup filled with wine glitters at night,
When the rallying pipa* summons us to fight.
Don't laugh if we lay drunk on battleground;
Any warriors ever came back safe and sound?

* pipa, a plucked string instrument with a fretted fingerboard; 4-stringed Chinese lute.

译后小记

《凉州词》是唐代诗人王翰的组诗作品之一。此词渲染了出征前盛大华贵的酒筵以及战士们痛快豪饮的场面，表现了战士们将生死置之度外的旷达、奔放的思想感情。

"葡萄美酒夜光杯",犹如突然间拉开帷幕,在人们的眼前展现出五光十色、琳琅满目、酒香四溢的盛大筵席。"欲饮琵琶马上催"是说正在大家准备畅饮之时,乐队也奏起了琵琶,"马上"二字,往往又使人联想到"出发",在西域胡人中,琵琶本来就是骑在马上弹奏的。"欲饮琵琶马上催",是着意渲染一种欢快宴饮的场面,也是催人振奋,鼓舞士气。为了诗意,笔者结合这两点,用 when 将一二行连起来译(The jade cup filled with wine glitters at night, / When the rallying pipa summons us to fight)。

词的最末两句"醉卧沙场君莫笑,古来征战几人回",顺着前两句的诗意来看应当是写筵席上的畅饮和劝酒,"古来征战几人回",显然是一种夸张的说法。两句结合起来译为 Don't laugh if we lay drunk on battleground;/Any warriors ever came back safe and sound?

译文力争再现原诗豪迈旷达之笔触,行尾押联韵 aabb。

46. 桃花溪

〔唐〕张旭

隐隐飞桥隔野烟,
石矶西畔问渔船。
桃花尽日随流水,
洞在清溪何处边。

46. Peach Blossom Brook

〔Tang Dynasty〕By Zhang Xu

A bridge shape is loomed out of the hazy mist;
A fishing boat is moored westside of a rocky-islet.
"Peach blossoms are drifting in the brook all day;
Do you know where is the entrance to the cave?"

译后小记

《桃花溪》是唐代书法家、诗人张旭借陶渊明《桃花源记》的意境而创作的写景诗。此诗通过描写桃花溪幽美的景色和作者对渔人的询问,抒写一种向往世外桃源,追求美好生活的心情。诗由远外落笔,写山谷深幽,迷离恍惚,隔烟朦胧,其境若仙;然后镜头移近,写桃花流水,渔舟轻泛,问讯渔人,寻找桃源。全诗构思婉曲,情韵悠长,创造了一个饶有画意、充满情趣的幽深境界。

翻译就是理解、表达和变通。译诗前两句具体写景（A bridge shape is loomed out of the hazy mist; A fishing boat moored westside of a rocky-islet）；后两句采用直接引语来问渔人（"Peach blossoms are drifting in the brook all day; Do you know where is the entrance to the cave?"）。原诗中"问渔船"不对应译诗中的具体表达，但其意自明。

47. 望月怀远

〔唐〕张九龄

海上生明月，
天涯共此时。
情人怨遥夜，
竟夕起相思。
灭烛怜光满，
披衣觉露滋。
不堪盈手赠，
还寝梦佳期。

47. *Yearning Under the Moon*

〔Tang Dynasty〕By Zhang Jiuling

A bright moon is born above the sea;
This moment I gaze at it afar with thee.
How could the moonlit night be so long?
The yearning between lovers so strong.
Candles snuffed, I see the moon full bright;
Coat on I stroll outside, a dew moist night.
Oh, I just can't hand thee the moonbeams
But go to bed to meet with thee in dreams.

译后小记

此诗是望月怀思的名篇。开头紧扣题目,首句写"望月",次句写"怀远";接着直抒对远方亲人的思念之情;五六句承接三四句,具体描绘了彻夜难眠的情境;结尾两句进一步抒写了对远方亲人的一片深情。

中文语篇往往视角流动,英文语篇往往视角固定,为了整个语篇的连贯,译文从"我"的视角来译,注重音韵效果及情感表达。

第五行,"灭烛"原用 blown out,改为 snuffed。

原诗是近体严格的五言律诗,译诗采用 aabbccdd 韵式,诗行中采用头韵或行中韵。

48. 西江夜行

〔唐〕张九龄

遥夜人何在，
澄潭月里行。
悠悠天宇旷，
切切故乡情。
外物寂无扰，
中流澹自清。
念归林叶换，
愁坐露华生。
犹有汀洲鹤，
宵分乍一鸣。

48. *The Night Voyage on Xijiang River*

〔Tang Dynasty〕By Zhang Jiuling

Where are you in this long, long night?
On clear river, the boat moves in moonlight.
The sky and field are empty and wide;
Bouts of homesickness come to mind.
The scenery around shows no sorrow;
The clear water of the river freely flows.
The trees have already changed their leaves;

Lost in nostalgia, I let dew wet my sleeves.
An abrupt bird cry splits up the dawn sky;
White cranes perch on the sandbar overnight.

译后小记

此诗描写西江月夜,淡雅宁静,别是一种境界。第一句说夜里起行,第二句说到思念故乡,第三句说到周围环境清寂无扰,第四句又是说到思乡,最后一句是诗词里面常用的手法,说到了早上鹤鸣一声,这句更反衬思乡情意。

"遥夜人何在",这里的"人",笔者用 you,指诗人思念的人;"澄潭"指西江水深清澈,"夜里行"的主语是船。"悠悠天宇旷,切切故乡情",这里前半句写外在的客观世界,后半句写诗人的心理世界,形成对比。"外物寂无扰,中流澹自清",这一句顺承"悠悠天宇旷",周围的万物并无悲伤,一切都是自然态;"念归林叶换,愁坐露华生",这一句顺承"切切故乡情",诗人沉浸于思念亲人,思念故乡,以至于露水打湿衣袖。"犹有汀洲鹤,宵分乍一鸣",不知不觉一夜过去,沙洲上的一声鹤鸣,将诗人从沉思中惊醒。

在理解诗意的基础上来表达,情与韵在字里行间,译诗行尾押联韵 aabbccddee,其中,个别为元音韵。

49. 感遇 · 其一

〔唐〕张九龄

兰叶春葳蕤，
桂华秋皎洁。
欣欣此生意，
自尔为佳节。
谁知林栖者，
闻风坐相悦。
草木有本心，
何求美人折！

49. *An Epiphany · Poem One*

〔Tang Dynasty〕By Zhang Jiuling

Spring orchids are in lush green;
Autumn osmanthus are bright clean.
Grass and trees are in a thriving scene;
Naturally it's the ever-best season.
Somehow, a hermit in the woods
Smells the scent in a jovial mood.
The flora with a unique nature would
Not to be picked or understood!

译后小记

《感遇·其一》是唐代诗人张九龄所作的一首五言诗。诗一开始用整齐的偶句,以春兰秋桂对举,点出无限生机和清雅高洁之特征。三四句,写兰桂充满活力却荣而不媚,不求人知之品质。上半首写兰桂,不写人。五六句以"谁知"急转引出与兰桂同调的山中隐者来。末两句点出无心与物相竞的情怀。

译诗采用了跨行诗句,在传达原诗诗意的基础上,追求一定的音韵效果。

50. 登鹳雀楼

〔唐〕王之涣

白日依山尽，
黄河入海流。
欲穷千里目，
更上一层楼。

50. *Ascending the Stork Tower*

〔Tang Dynasty〕By Wang Zhihuan

By distant hills the sun is homing;
Towards sea Yellow River is flowing.
If you'd enjoy a grander sight,
Please climb to a greater height.

译后小记

此诗前两句写的是自然景色，但开笔就有缩万里于咫尺，使咫尺有万里之势；后两句写意，写得出人意料，把哲理与景物、情势溶化得天衣无缝，成为鹳雀楼上一首不朽的绝唱。

原诗前两句对仗工整，译诗用同样的句型译出（By distant hills the sun is homing; / Towards sea Yellow River is flowing），并采用拟人手法

来译"白日依山尽"(the sun is homing);第三句为假设,第四句为祈使句,为减少命令口吻带来的不悦,译文加了 please 一词。译诗行尾押联韵 aabb。

51. 瑶池

〔唐〕李商隐

瑶池阿母绮窗开，
黄竹歌声动地哀。
八骏日行三万里，
穆王何事不重来。

51. *Jade Pool*

〔Tang Dynasty〕By Li Shangyin

The Queen of the West Heaven in Jade Pool opened a window,
Only to hear mournful music played solemn, a world of sorrow!
King Mu had an eight-horse carriage for 30,000 miles a day,
But what prevent him to keep his promise of coming again?

译后小记

此诗是借西王母与周穆王相约见面的传说来构思的。作者抓住西王母希望穆王"复来"、穆王也许诺复来这一点，虚构了一个西王母盼望穆王归来的情节，讥刺皇帝求仙的虚妄。

此诗翻译有不少需要推敲的词："阿母"，西王母，笔者译为 The Queen of the West Heaven；"瑶池"，传说中西王母居住的地方，笔者译为 Jade Pool；"黄竹歌声"，源自典故：周穆王作《黄竹诗》三章以哀民,后以"黄竹"比喻关心民瘼,应制诗中多代指皇帝诗作,诗中不便过多解释或加注,笔者意译为mournful music;"八骏"是以部分代整体的认知转换,不是八匹骏马,而是指骏马和座驾(包括八匹骏马和马车),故笔者译为an eight-horse carriage。

在完全理解原诗基础上来表达,译诗注意音韵节奏。

52. 春晓

〔唐〕孟浩然

春眠不觉晓，
处处闻啼鸟。
夜来风雨声，
花落知多少。

52. *Spring Dawn*

〔Tang Dynasty〕By Meng Haoran

It's dawn before I know;
Birds chirp high and low.
Overnight wind and showers
Have blown off many flowers.

译后小记

此诗是唐代诗人孟浩然隐居在鹿门山时所作，诗人抓住春天的早晨刚刚醒来时的一瞬间展开联想，描绘了一幅春天早晨的绚丽图景，抒发了诗人热爱春天、珍惜春光的美好心情。

诗题"春晓"，笔者译为 Spring Dawn，意谓春天早晨天刚破晓之时，有那么半个时辰，鸟儿会叽叽喳喳欢快鸣叫，不宜译为 Spring Morning，因为 morning 的时间跨度太长，不确切。

首句破题，写春睡的香甜，也流露着对朝阳明媚的喜爱；次句写景，写悦耳的春声，也交代了醒来的原因。首句"春眠不觉晓"，这里包含了两个主谓结构"春晓"与"觉晓"，译者用 before 加以连接。第二句"处处闻啼鸟"，"处处"，笔者用 high and low，而不采用 everywhere，因为鸟儿婉转枝头高高低低；"啼鸟"，笔者用 chirp 更显鸟儿的欢快。

第三、第四句"夜来风雨声，花落知多少"转为写回忆，末句又回到眼前，由喜春返为惜春，表示对前一晚风雨摧花的感慨。

译诗音韵和谐，行尾押完全韵 aabb。

53. 初秋

〔唐〕孟浩然

不觉初秋夜渐长,
清风习习重凄凉。
炎炎暑退茅斋静,
阶下丛莎有露光。

53. *Early Autumn*

〔Tang Dynasty〕By Meng Haoran

The night becomes longer before I know;
It's gloomy again as cool breezes blow.
The sweltering summer fades; silent is my shed
With glittering dew on grass below the step.

译后小记

此诗好译,唯有几处分享,"不觉"译者采用 before I know;"清风习习"译为 cool breezes blow。译诗尽量流畅自然,五音步抑扬格为主旋律,行尾押联韵 aabb,前两行为完全韵,后两行为元音韵。

54. 渡浙江问舟中人

〔唐〕孟浩然

潮落江平未有风，
扁舟共济与君同。
时时引领望天末，
何处青山是越中。

54. *Asking the Peers While Crossing the Qiantang River*

〔Tang Dynasty〕By Meng Haoran

The tide ebbs, with no wind, the river is still.
"Luck brings us to the same boat, young men!"
I crane my neck and look afar time and again,
"But do you know which is Shaoxing's hill?"

译后小记

"浙江"，即钱塘江，译为 the Qiantang River，既清楚明了，又可免与省名的"浙江"混淆；"越中"，指现在的"绍兴"，可照译 Shaoxing。

诗题"渡浙江问舟中人"中的"舟中人"，笔者理解为同坐一船的人，译为 peer；既是"问舟中人"，笔者将诗中"扁舟共济与君同"和

"何处青山是越中"转化为直接引语,似乎是诗人直接发问舟中人,更有现场情景体验感。"Luck brings us to the same boat, young men!"(真是幸运咱们同船共度,年轻人!)是不是很亲切,很符合当时诗人的口吻呢?

第三句"时时引领望天末",笔者译为 I crane my neck and look afar time and again。"引领"译为 crane my neck,是不是很生动形象?look afar 是不是"望天末"?time and again 是笔者加上的,是不是符合当时诗人的心情和实际情况呢?

翻译诗歌,笔者注重情景体验感,译诗自然流畅,行尾押抱韵 abba。

55. 菊花

〔唐〕元稹

秋丛绕舍似陶家,
遍绕篱边日渐斜。
不是花中偏爱菊,
此花开尽更无花。

55. *Chrysanthemums*

〔Tang Dynasty〕By Yuan Zhen

It seems Tao's home lying in autumn blooms;
I stroll around the fence till the dusk looms.
Not that I'm partial to chrysanthemum flower;
But there is no blossom to admire thereafter.

译后小记

诗中三处提到菊花,译者采用三种不同译法,题目"菊花"用的是全称 Chrysanthemums,诗文中第一句"秋丛"译为 autumn blooms,第三句"菊"译为 mum flowers,一是为了避免重复,二是为了减少音节,三是为了音韵效果。

"陶家"指东晋后期的大诗人陶渊明,陶渊明一生爱菊,写过多首与菊相关的诗歌,如"采菊东篱下,悠然见南山"是千年以来脍炙人口的名句。"陶家"译为英语Tao's；"秋丛绕舍"，译者转换视角，以陶舍为中心，译为…Tao's home lying in autumn blooms，如果译为…Tao's home surrounded by autumn blooms，则此句略显冗长。

译诗第二行转换视角，"日渐斜"转换为"直到黄昏逼近"，译为till the dusk looms，换言之，"我一直绕篱赏菊直到黄昏"。

以诗译诗，极力保持原诗的画面自然流畅，兼顾音韵效果。

56. 菩提偈

〔唐〕慧能

菩提本无树,
明镜亦非台,
本来无一物,
何处惹尘埃?

56. *Bodhi Verse*

〔Tang Dynasty〕Huineng

There is no Bodhi tree at all;
Nor a bright mirror platform.
Neither is a specific object;
Where does the dust befall?

译后小记

此诗意在说明一切有为法皆如梦幻泡影,教人不要妄想执着,才能明心见性,自证菩提。"菩提"原本比喻智慧,"明镜"比喻清心。

此诗翻译的难点在于理解原诗,诗中的倒装句不容易识解,"菩提本无树"为"本无菩提树"的倒装句;"明镜亦非台"为"亦非明镜台"的倒装句。"菩提树"(智慧)和"明镜台"(清心)都不是具体的物件,怎么会有尘埃呢?

翻译就是理解,表达,变通。在追求音韵之前,先求诗意、禅意。

57. 回归自我

〔唐〕无尽藏

终日寻春不见春，
芒鞋踏破岭头云。
归来偶把梅花嗅，
春在枝头已十分。

57. Return Back to Who I Am

〔Tang Dynasty〕By Wujincang

I've been seeking spring in vain all day
With footprints all over mountain way.
A sudden scent of plum blooms by chance,
I find spring has already come onto branch.

译后小记

无尽藏，佛教语，谓佛德广大无边，作用于万物，无穷无尽。诗的作者无尽藏，是一位比丘尼的法号，不是姓名，故诗人法号音译为Wujincang。诗人相传为六祖慧能八拜之交刘志略的姑姑——无尽藏，唐代武周时尼姑，俗姓刘，韶州（今广东韶关）人，曾向六祖慧能问经义。

诗文中寻春不见春，而春已然在枝头，人生又岂不是如此道理。

原诗短小精悍，富于哲思，音韵流畅。翻译不是译字，"芒鞋""归来"在译文中没有对应的单词，"芒鞋"转换为"足迹"（footprints），"归来"省略没译。

译诗尽量接近其风格，行尾韵为 aabb，前两行为完全韵，后两行为不完全韵。

58. 渔歌子

〔唐〕张志和

西塞山前白鹭飞,
桃花流水鳜鱼肥。
青箬笠,
绿蓑衣,
斜风细雨不须归。

58. *A Fisherman's Song*

〔Tang Dynasty〕Zhang Zhihe

In front of the hill, egrets soar high and low;
In peach bloom stream mandarin fish grow.
A bamboo hat blue,
A straw cloak green,
He enjoys fishing in the zephyr and rain.

译后小记

《渔歌子》是唐代诗人张志和的一首词,诗人假借渔夫生活来表现自己隐居生活的乐趣。

"西塞山前"点明地点,"白鹭"是闲适的象征,写白鹭自在地飞翔,衬托渔夫的悠闲自得。"桃花流水鳜鱼肥"意思是说:桃花盛开,江水猛涨，这时节鳜鱼长得正肥。桃红与水绿相映，表现暮春西塞山前的湖光山色，渲染了渔夫的生活环境。"青箬笠，绿蓑衣，斜风细雨不须归"，描写了渔夫捕鱼的情态。渔夫头戴青箬笠，身穿绿蓑衣，在斜风细雨中乐而忘归。

西塞山，在浙江省湖州市西面，简单译为 the hill。"斜风"指微风，和风，故将"斜风细雨"译为 zephyr and rain。

此诗在翻译过程中，选词注意诗人的情感基调，贴近原词风格。

59. 以退为进

〔后梁〕契此

手把青秧插满田，
低头便见水中天。
心地清净方为道，
退步原来是向前。

59. *Regressing to Progress*

〔the Later Liang Dynasty〕Qi Ci

Seedlings in hand, I stoop to plant the rice;
With lowering head, I see in water the sky.
A simple truth inspires my peaceful mind:
Regress is making progress sometimes, aye!

译后小记

这是五代后梁时的契此和尚创作的一首古风绝句，此诗又名《插秧诗》。契此俗姓张，又称"布袋和尚"，号长汀子，唐末至五代后梁时期明州奉化(现浙江省宁波市奉化区)僧人，是五代时后梁高僧。此诗中契此和尚通过退步插秧的情境来阐述参禅的境界。

诗题"以退为进"采用动名词短语 regressing 和表目的的不定式 to progress 来译；"青秧"即秧苗，译为 seedlings，"青"不译；"弯腰"译为 stoop(弯腰；俯身) 倒也契合；"心地清净"转换为"清净心地"来译为 peaceful mind，"道"是中国文化概念词汇，无英语对等词，这里根据语境译为"truth"。

译诗尚且自然流畅，轻重音节按常态分布，主流格律为抑扬格五音步，行尾押韵格式为 abcb。

原诗格律分析如下：

Seedlings in hand, I stoop to plant the rice;
With lowering head, I see in water the sky.
A simple truth inspires my peaceful mind;
Regress is making progress sometimes, aye!

60. 梅

〔宋〕王安石

墙角数枝梅,
凌寒独自开。
遥知不是雪,
为有暗香来。

60. *Plum Blossom*

〔Song Dynasty〕Wang Anshi

A few plums at the corner loom
Against the bitter cold alone abloom.
From afar I make out they're not snow
Cause wafts of faint fragrance flow.

译后小记

《梅》是北宋诗人王安石创作的一首五言绝句。此诗前两句写墙角梅花不惧严寒,傲然独放;后两句写梅花的幽香,以梅拟人,凌寒独开,比喻品格高贵,暗香沁人。亦是以梅花的坚强和高洁品格,喻示那些像诗人一样,处于艰难环境中依然能坚持操守、主张正义的人。

"墙角数枝梅","墙角"不引人注目,不易为人所知,更未被人赏识,却又毫不在乎,故将词句译为 A few plums at the corner loom,正常语序是 A few plums loom at the corner(墙角处隐约可见几枝梅)。

"凌寒独自开",这里没写梅花的姿态,而只写它"独自开",突出梅花不畏寒,故译为 against the bitter cold alone abloom(迎着严寒,独自绽放),作上句的补充说明。

"遥知不是雪",意谓远远望去十分纯净洁白,但知道不是雪而是梅花,译为 From afar I make out it's not snow,"为有暗香来"(Cause wafts of faint fragrance flow)。

译诗流畅自然,行尾押完全韵 aabb。

61. 泊船瓜洲

〔宋〕王安石

京口瓜洲一水间，
钟山只隔数重山。
春风又绿江南岸，
明月何时照我还。

61. *Moored at Melon Islet*

〔Song Dynasty〕By Wang Anshi

The River severs the islet from south shore;
A few mountains away is my home door.
Spring wind greens the south shore again;
When will the moon shine me back, when?

译后小记

《泊船瓜洲》是北宋文学家王安石创作的一首七言绝句。诗中首句通过写京口和瓜洲距离之短及船行之快，流露出一种轻松、愉悦的心情；第二句写诗人回望居住地钟山，产生依依不舍之情；第三句描写了春意盎然的江南景色；最后以疑问语气结尾，再一次强调了对故乡的思念。

"京口"，在今江苏省镇江市，长江的南岸，与瓜洲相对；"瓜洲",在今天江苏省扬州市邗(hán)江区县南,与京口相对;"一水",指长江。诗歌翻译,意境重要,这么复杂的地名,笔者加以简化,the River 指长江,诗题中的"瓜州"译为 Melon Islet,诗文中再提及就用 the islet;"京口"即下文"南岸",译为 south shore。

首句"京口瓜洲一水间"(The River severs the islet from south shore)写了望中之景,诗人站在瓜洲渡口,放眼南望,看到了南边岸上的"京口"与"瓜洲"这么近,中间隔一条江水。

次句"钟山只隔数重山",诗人第一次罢相后即寓居江宁钟山,"只隔"两字极言钟山之近在咫尺,故译为 A few mountains away lies my home door。

"春风又绿江南岸"(Spring wind greens the south shore again),"明月何时照我还"(When will the moon shine me back, when?),诗人以设问句式表达想法。

译诗流畅自然,行尾押韵 aabb。

62. 饮湖上初晴后雨

〔宋〕苏轼

水光潋滟晴方好，
山色空蒙雨亦奇。
欲把西湖比西子，
淡妆浓抹总相宜。

62. *Drinking on Lake, Sunny First Then Rainy*

〔Song Dynasty〕By Su Shi

The glinting ripples in sun, a sight so fair;
The cloudy hills in rain, a scene so rare.
I want to compare Lake West to Lady West;
Be gaily or plainly dressed, she is best.

译后小记

这是一首赞美西湖美景的诗。此诗不是描写西湖的一处之景、一时之景，而是对西湖美景的全面描写概括品评，尤其是后二句，被认为是对西湖的恰当评语。

"水光潋滟晴方好"（The glinting ripples in sun, a sight so fair）描写西湖晴天的水光：在灿烂的阳光照耀下，西湖水波荡漾，波光闪闪，十分美丽。

"山色空濛雨亦奇"(The cloudy hills in rain, a scene so rare)描写雨天的山色:在雨幕笼罩下,西湖周围的群山,迷迷茫茫,若有若无,非常奇妙。

译诗在表达原诗诗意基础上,有一定音韵节奏,主流旋律为抑扬格五音步,行尾押韵 aabb,第四行有行中元音韵 gaily 与 plainly,dressed 与 best。

译诗格律分析如下:

The gl<u>i</u>nting r<u>i</u>pples in s<u>u</u>n, a s<u>i</u>ght so f<u>ai</u>r;
The cl<u>ou</u>dy h<u>i</u>lls in r<u>ai</u>n, a sc<u>e</u>ne so r<u>a</u>re.
I want comp<u>a</u>re Lake W<u>e</u>st to L<u>a</u>dy W<u>e</u>st;
Be g<u>ai</u>ly or pl<u>ai</u>nly dr<u>e</u>ssed, sh<u>e</u> is b<u>e</u>st.

63. 赠刘景文

〔宋〕苏轼

荷尽已无擎雨盖,
菊残犹有傲霜枝。
一年好景君须记,
最是橙黄橘绿时。

63. *To Liu Jingwen*

〔Song Dynasty〕By Su Shi

The lotuses wither with drooping leaves;
The daisies fade with proud twigs still seen.
Remember greatest scene of the year, please;
Oranges are orange, tangerines green.

译后小记

《赠刘景文》又名《冬景》,是北宋文学家苏轼赠刘景文的一首七言绝句。这首诗作于元祐五年(1090年),是送给好友刘景文的一首勉励诗。此诗前半首说"荷尽菊残"仍要保持傲雪冰霜的气节,后半首通过"橙黄橘绿"来勉励朋友困难只是一时,乐观向上,切莫意志消沉,抒发作者的广阔胸襟和对同处窘境中友人的劝勉和支持,托物言志,意境高远。

荷尽：荷花枯萎；擎雨盖：托住雨珠的叶子；"荷尽已无擎雨盖"，荷叶枯萎，耷拉着叶子，drooping leaves 是"擎雨盖"的意象再造；菊残犹有傲霜枝(The daisies fade with proud twigs still seen)，基本是直译；"一年好景君须记"(Remember greatest scene of the year, please)，注意英语中少用教训口吻 You should remember 之类；"最是橙黄橘绿时"(Oranges are orange, tangerines green) 承接第三句，译文省略了一个 are。

译文流畅自然表达诗意，各行押韵 abab。

64. 题西林壁

〔宋〕苏轼

横看成岭侧成峰,
远近高低各不同。
不识庐山真面目,
只缘身在此山中。

64. A Poem Inscribed on the Wall of Xilin Temple

〔Song Dynasty〕By Su Shi

It looks a ridge from front, a peak from side,
Different angles, far and near, a different sight.
The true face of Lushan does always hide
Simply cause in the very mountain I reside.

译后小记

这是一首诗中有画的写景诗,又是一首哲理诗,哲理蕴含在对庐山景色的描绘之中。

"横看成岭侧成峰,远近高低各不同"说的是游人从远处、近处、高处、低处等不同角度观察庐山面貌是可以得到不同观感的。有时你看到的是起伏连绵的山岭,有时你看到的是高耸入云端的山峰。这两句概括而形象地写出了移步换形、千姿万态的庐山风景。

　　首句"横看成岭侧成峰",笔者理解"横看"是从前面看,故有首句译文 It looks a ridge from front, a peak from side;"远近高低"是指不同视角,故有译文 Different angles, far and near, a different sight。"不识庐山真面目"逻辑主语是"我",译文转换视角,以"庐山"为主语,译为 The true face of Lushan does always hide, 这样译似乎庐山总是犹抱琵琶半遮面,更具诗意,紧接第四句 Simply cause in the very mountain I reside, 这样译语意连贯。

　　译诗表意完整,有一定音韵节奏,行尾押韵 abaa。

65. 定风波·莫听穿林打叶声

〔宋〕苏轼

莫听穿林打叶声,
何妨吟啸且徐行。
竹杖芒鞋轻胜马,
谁怕?
一蓑烟雨任平生。

料峭春风吹酒醒,
微冷,
山头斜照却相迎。
回首向来萧瑟处,
归去,
也无风雨也无晴。

65. Calming the Waves · Listen Not to the Rain Pattering the Leaves

〔Song Dynasty〕By Su Shi

Listen not to the rain pattering the leaves.
Why not slow down and chant at ease?
Sandals on foot, a cane in hand, I'm a swift steed;
Who feels scared?

A coir cloak in drizzling rain, I enjoy my life indeed.

I am sobered by the cool spring breeze,
A sense of freeze;
A slanting sun atop the mountain is in season.
Looking back at the bleak track,
I shall go back!
I don't care wind, rain or sunshine, no reason.

译后小记

  这首记事抒怀之词作于1082年(宋神宗元丰五年)春,当时是苏轼因"乌台诗案"被贬为黄州(今湖北黄冈)团练副使的第三个春天。词人与朋友春日出游,风雨忽至,朋友深感狼狈,词人却毫不在乎,泰然处之,吟咏自若,缓步而行。上阕着眼于雨中,下阕着眼于雨后,全词体现出一个正直文人在坎坷人生中力求解脱之道,表现出旷达超脱的胸襟。

  原词工整易懂,上阕押韵 aabba,下阕押韵 aaabba。译词较好再现原词意境,有一定音韵效果。译词上阕押韵 aabcb,下阕押韵 aabccb。

66. 山村咏怀

〔宋〕邵康节

一去二三里，
烟村四五家，
亭台六七座，
八九十枝花。

66. A Lyric of a Mountain Village

〔Song Dynasty〕By Shao Kangjie

In a moment, two or three miles go by,
Whips of smoke from chimneys four or five
Come in sight as well as pavilions six or seven
Dotted with flowers eight or nine, oh, ten!

译后小记

《山村咏怀》是北宋哲学家邵康节所作的一首诗。这首诗通过列锦的表现手法把烟村、人家、亭台、鲜花等景象排列在一起，构成一幅田园风光图，并创造出一种淡雅的意境，表达出诗人对大自然的喜爱与赞美之情。

诗中有"一至十"十个数字，笔者觉得有必要译出，结合排列景象，用流畅自然的一句话来译，不失原诗之诗味和意境，行尾押韵 aabb。

67. 生查子·元夕

〔宋〕欧阳修

去年元夜时,
花市灯如昼。
月上柳梢头,
人约黄昏后。

今年元夜时,
月与灯依旧。
不见去年人,
泪湿春衫袖。

67. Song of Hawthorn · Lantern Festival

〔Song Dynasty〕By Ouyang Xiu

Last year on Lantern Festival night,
Lanterns in fair shone as daylight.
The moon climbed on the willow;
We dated in twilight fairly mellow.

This year on Lantern Festival night,
The moon and lanterns still shine bright.
Where is the one who I dated last year?

Sleeves of my blouse are soaked in tears.

译后小记

　　词的上阕写去年元夜情事。"去年元夜时，花市灯如昼"写元宵之夜的繁华热闹，为下文情人的出场渲染出一种柔情的氛围。"月上柳梢头，人约黄昏后"情景交融，写出了恋人在月光柳影下两情依依、情话绵绵的景象，制造出朦胧清幽、婉约柔美的意境。下阕写今年元夜相思之苦。"月与灯依旧"与"不见去年人"相对照，引出"泪湿春衫袖"这一旧情难续的沉重哀伤，表达出词人对昔日恋人的一往情深。

　　译文中的 fairly mellow（飘飘然），根据上下文语境添加。上阕用过去时态，下阕用现在时态。

　　译诗主旋律为抑扬格四音步，行尾押韵 aabb aacc。

68. 虞美人·寄公度

〔宋〕舒亶

芙蓉落尽天涵水，

日暮沧波起。

背飞双燕贴云寒，

独向小楼东畔倚阑看。

浮生只合尊前老，

雪满长安道。

故人早晚上高台，

赠我江南春色一枝梅。

68. Beautiful Lady Yu · To My Friend, Gongdu

〔Song Dynasty〕By Shu Dan

With lotus shedding all its leaves, the sky and water merge into one sight,

And mists rise from water surface in twilight.

Close to clouds two swallows are flying apart;

Alone I board the pavilion and lean on the east hurdle gazing afar.

My lonesome hour shall run out in wine lonely;

Capital Chang'an is covered with snow deeply.

My friend shall ascend a height in morn or eve too,

And send me from the Southern in early spring a plum bloom.

译后小记

此词上片写景,借萧瑟秋色、分飞双燕暗喻别离之苦。下片抒情,用陆凯赠梅典故,表达彼此的深情厚谊和渴望相见的迫切心情。

原文"酒樽"隐喻"酒",这是以器具指代内容,故译文略去"樽"不译;"长安道"指代当时的帝都"长安","道"为与"老"押韵,没确切意义,故只译"长安",并补充文化信息"首都";"江南"简单译为 the Southern。

翻译此词时,笔者注重意境,不以形害意,用流畅自然的语言来表达原词,不限于字数,如首句"芙蓉落尽天涵水"(With lotus shedding all its leaves, the sky and water merge into one sight)无以复减。原文为长短句,译文也音步多少不一;原词上下两片尾字韵式都是前两句押仄声韵,后两句押平声韵,译文行尾押不完全韵 aabb ccdd。

69. 长相思·吴山青

〔宋〕林逋

吴山青,
越山青,
两岸青山相对迎,
谁知离别情。

君泪盈,
妾泪盈,
罗带同心结未成,
江边潮已平。

69. *Everlasting Longing · Wu Hills Green*

〔Song Dynasty〕By Lin Bu

Wu hills green,
Yue hills green,
The hills each side wave hello.
Who knows th'parting souls?

You're in tears;
I'm in tears.
Two loving hearts lack the knot;
The tides low offshore.

译后小记

  此词为一女子与情人诀别的情景，运用回环咏唱即民歌中常见的复沓形式，以回旋往复、一唱三叹的节奏和清新优美的语言，以一个女子的身份、口气，抒写了她因爱情生活受到破坏，被迫与心上人在江边诀别的悲怀。全词上片起兴，点明送别，下片写情，寄托离恨。

  此词翻译，笔者在紧贴原词语义的基础上，尝试一个音节对应一个汉字来译。

  吴山和越山耸立在钱塘江的北岸和南岸，笔者直译为 Wu hills, Yue hills，没有相关地理位置的补充。"两岸青山相对迎，谁知离别情"，吴山越山两两相对，隔江呼应，却是不懂恋人分别的愁绪，译为 The hills each side wave hello. / Who knows th' parting souls? 算是与原意接近吧。

  "罗带同心结未成，江边潮已平。"指钱江潮过后水面已经恢复平静了，两个没办法在一起的人心冷了，译为 Two loving hearts lack the knot; The tides low offshore。值得注意的是"江边潮已平"，是落潮，而非涨潮。

  译文一个音节对应一个汉字，语义与原词同，行尾押不完全韵 aabb，算是试验成功，但这种体验不可多得。

70. 一剪梅·红藕香残玉簟秋

〔宋〕李清照

红藕香残玉簟秋。
轻解罗裳，
独上兰舟。
云中谁寄锦书来？
雁字回时，
月满西楼。

花自飘零水自流。
一种相思，
两处闲愁。
此情无计可消除，
才下眉头，
却上心头。

70. *A Twig of Plum Blossoms · Lotus Flowers Fade, Bamboo Mats Cold*

〔Song Dynasty〕By Li Qingzhao

Lotus flowers fade, bamboo mats cold.
Gently taking off the silk coat,
Alone I am on a small boat.
From the cloud, who has sent me a line?

The moment the wild geese fly back aligned,
West chamber is bathed in moonlight.

Flower fades and falls, water flows, all by itself.
The same nostalgia
In two different places.
To eliminate this feeling is in vain;
This moment it leaves my brow,
Next moment it comes upon my mind.

译后小记

　　此词作于词人与丈夫赵明诚离别之后，寄寓着词人不忍离别的一腔深情，反映出初婚少妇沉溺于情海之中的纯洁心灵。全词以女性特有的沉挚情感，丝毫"不落俗套"的表现方式，展示出一种婉约之美，格调清新，意境幽美，称得上是一首工致精巧的别情佳作。

　　原词幽美，笔者尽力为之，在传达原义的基础上，追求一定的音韵之美。

71. 夏日绝句

〔宋〕李清照

生当作人杰，
死亦为鬼雄。
至今思项羽，
不肯过江东。

71. A Quatrain in Summer

〔Song Dynasty〕By Li Qingzhao

Be it alive, one should be a great hero!
Be it dead, one should be a great ghost!
I still miss Xiang Yu* who chose to fight,
Rather than survive at the other riverside.

* Xiang Yu (232 BC—202 BC), a famous general of the State of Chu (1115 BC—223 BC).

译后小记

这是词人李清照创作的一首五言绝句，是一首借古讽今、抒发悲愤的怀古诗。诗的前两句，语出惊人，直抒胸臆，提出人"生当作人杰"，为国建功立业，报效朝廷；"死"也应该做"鬼雄"，方才不愧于顶天立地的好男儿。深深的爱国之情喷涌而出，震撼人心。最后两句，诗人通过歌颂项羽的悲壮之举来讽刺南宋当权者不思进取、苟且偷生的无耻行径。全诗只有短短的二十个字，却连用三个典故。

人杰：人中的豪杰。汉高祖曾称赞开国功臣张良、萧何、韩信是"人杰"。

鬼雄：鬼中的英雄。屈原《国殇》："身既死兮神以灵，子魂魄兮为鬼雄。"

项羽：秦末时自立为西楚霸王，与刘邦争夺天下，在垓下之战中，兵败自杀。

江东：项羽当初随叔父项梁起兵的地方。

前两个典故，译者略去文化背景，采取意译，生时应当做人中豪杰，死后也要做鬼中英雄(Be it alive, one should be a great hero! Be it dead, one should be a great ghost!)。

第三个典故，译者采取了加注，补充文化背景。

72. 如梦令·昨夜雨疏风骤

〔宋〕李清照

昨夜雨疏风骤,
浓睡不消残酒。
试问卷帘人,
却道海棠依旧。
知否,
知否?
应是绿肥红瘦

72. *A Dreamy Song · The Wind Whistled with Little Rain Last Night*

〔Song Dynasty〕By Li Qingzhao

The wind whistled with little rain last night;
A sound sleep after a drink, I still feel tired.
I ask the maid to roll up the curtain,
"Begonia," replies she, "the same as before".
"Oh, don't you know?
Don't you know?
The red should fade, while the green should grow more."

译后小记

　　此词借宿酒醒后询问花事的描写，委婉地表达了作者怜花惜花的心情。全词篇幅虽短，但含蓄蕴藉，对人物心理情绪的刻画栩栩如生。后人对此词评价甚高，尤其是"绿肥红瘦"一句，更为历代文人所赞赏。

　　雨疏风骤：雨点稀疏，晚风急猛。译者用了 whistle 一词来将风"骤"具体化。

　　浓睡不消残酒：虽然睡了一夜，仍有余醉未消。浓睡：酣睡，译为 a sound sleep；残酒：尚未消散的醉意，诗人应是还有疲乏倦怠之感，故译为 feel tired。

　　绿肥红瘦：绿叶繁茂，红花凋零。

　　原词押韵工整，格式为 aabacca，译文押韵格式为 aabcddc。

73. 夜书所见

〔宋〕叶绍翁

萧萧梧叶送寒声,
江上秋风动客情。
知有儿童挑促织,
夜深篱落一灯明。

73. *Nostalgia Sights on a Lonely Night*

〔the Southern Song Dynasty〕By Ye Shaoweng

The rustling parasol leaves a chilly sound;
The whistled wind over river stirs my mind.
I know the kids are catching crickets round;
A flicking light by hedge at night I find.

译后小记

《夜书所见》是南宋诗人叶绍翁所作的七言古诗。诗一二两句写景,借落叶飘飞、秋风瑟瑟、寒气袭人烘托游子漂泊流浪、孤单寂寞的凄凉之感。三四两句写儿童夜捉蟋蟀,兴致高昂,巧妙地反衬悲情,更显客居他乡的孤寂无奈。该诗以景衬情,动静结合,以梧叶声和风声衬出秋夜的寂静,还运用了对比手法,以儿童夜捉促织的乐景反衬自己客居他乡的悲情。

首句"萧萧梧叶送寒声"译为独立词组 The rustling parasol leaves a chilly sound。leaves 是名词"树叶";此句"江上秋风动客情","动"也颇有意思,笔者用 stir 一词,来表达萧瑟秋风起,"我"不由心感凄凉。三四句以儿童挑灯捕捉蟋蟀的欢快情景反衬作者对家人的思念之情。

译诗主流格律为五音步抑扬格,押韵 abab,格律分析如下:

The rustling parasol leaves a chilly sound;
The whistled wind over river stirs my mind.
I know the kids are catching crickets round;
A flicking light by hedge at night I find.

74. 初秋

〔宋〕俞桂

火老金柔暑告残,
乘凉正好望西山。
秋声来处无寻觅,
只作窗前竹叶间。

74. *Early Autumn*

〔the Southern Song Dynasty〕By Yu Gui

Summer heat is fading like embers of a fire still;
No way to seek cool, I've to look far into the hill.
The sound of autumn comes, but no one knows
Except the bamboo leaves before the windows.

译后小记

炎夏已去,初秋已至,然余热未消。作者从西山、竹叶之间来寻觅秋的味道,以小见大,表现出作者对秋天的热爱。

唐代诗人韩愈和孟郊的《纳凉联句》:"金柔气尚低,火老候愈浊。"

宋代诗人杨万里的《夏夜露坐》诗之一:"火老殊未热,雨多还自晴。"

由此可见,"火老金柔暑告残"指残夏,也是人们常说的秋老虎,故译为 Summer heat is fading like embers of a fire still。

"乘凉正好望西山"(No way to seek cool, I've to look far into the hill),这还是在夏天的尾巴,所以还需要乘凉纳凉。这里"西山"是否也可以是"东山"、"南山"或"北山"呢?故翻译时,笔者只译了"山"。

"秋声来处无寻觅,只作窗前竹叶间。"(The sound of autumn comes, but no one knows / Except the bamboo leaves before the windows.)这是傍晚的风,带着一丝丝风意。秋气若有还无,也只是在那微微晃动的竹叶里。

行尾押完全韵 aabb。

75. 除夜雪

〔南宋〕陆游

北风吹雪四更初,
嘉瑞天教及岁除。
半盏屠苏犹未举,
灯前小草写桃符。

75. Snow on New Year's Eve

〔the Southern Song Dynasty〕By Lu You

North wind wafts snow at midnight New Year's Eve;
Godsend snow promises a good beginning I believe.
Half a glass of Tusu Wine is not yet raised to celebrate;
By lamp I'm hurry to write Spring Festival couplets.

译后小记

这首诗有很多文化缺省的词汇,比如,四更、瑞雪、岁除、屠苏酒、草体字、桃符等。

"四更初",指"四更天:丑时,01:00—03:00"之初,即 01:00 稍过时分,可以译为 midnight。"午夜:一般指 12:00—2:00 之间"。"嘉瑞"是瑞雪;"天教"是天赐,可译为 godsend;"岁除"是除夕(除夜)。

屠苏酒,是在中国古代春节时饮用的酒品,故又名岁酒。屠苏是古代的一种房屋，因为是在这种房子里酿的酒，所以称为屠苏酒。据说屠苏酒是汉末名医华佗创制而成的，具有益气温阳、祛风散寒、避除疫疠之邪的功效。这么复杂的文化背景，笔者只能音译处理，译为Tusu Wine。

在宋代，桃符已经由纸张代替桃木板，称之为"春联"或者"春贴纸"。故诗中的桃符理解为"春联"，译为Spring Festival couplets。再如王安石的《元日》："爆竹声中一岁除，春风送暖入屠苏；千门万户曈曈日，总把新桃换旧符。"

此诗翻译，能用流畅自然的语言真实再现原诗已是不易，不强求全诗押韵。

76. 游山西村

〔南宋〕陆游

莫笑农家腊酒浑,
丰年留客足鸡豚。
山重水复疑无路,
柳暗花明又一村。
箫鼓追随春社近,
衣冠简朴古风存。
从今若许闲乘月,
拄杖无时夜叩门。

76. *A Visit to the Village of Shanxi*

〔the Southern Song Dynasty〕By Lu You

Don't laugh at the farmer his wine far from mellow;
In a bumper year, he keeps best dish for his fellow.
The twists and turns of the hills and rills are followed
By another village among the flowers and willows.
Flutes blowing, drums playing, Spring Day is near;
The simple ancient custom is still preserved here.
From now on, If I can idle around in moonlight,
On crutches, I'd knock on your door at night time.

译后小记

这是一首纪游抒情诗，是陆游的名篇之一。抒写江南农村日常生活，诗人紧扣诗题"游"字，但又不具体描写游村的过程，而是剪取游村的见闻，来体现不尽之游兴。全诗首写诗人出游到农家，次写村外之景物，复写村中之情事，末写频来夜游。

此诗中有不少文化概念词，是翻译难点。

腊酒：腊月里酿造的酒。

足鸡豚(tún)：意思是准备了丰盛的菜肴。豚，小猪，诗中代指猪肉。

"酒浑"，如何译，笔者反面照笔，译为 far from mellow(不够醇厚)；"丰年"，bumper year；"山重水复"：一座座山、一道道水重重叠叠，笔者用两对押头韵的词来译为 the twists and turns of the hills and rills；"柳暗花明"，柳色深绿，花色红艳，译为 the flowers and willows；"箫鼓"：吹箫打鼓，译为 Flutes blowing, drums playing；"春社"：古代把立春后第五个戊日作为春社日，拜祭社公(土地神)和五谷神，祈求丰收，笔者略去文化背景，译为 Spring Day。

译诗行尾押元音韵 aabbccdd。

77. 示儿

〔南宋〕陆游

死去元知万事空，
但悲不见九州同。
王师北定中原日，
家祭无忘告乃翁。

77. *To My Son*

〔the Southern Song Dynasty〕By Lu You

All will be void when I should die.
Woe! The homeland is yet to be united.
When the royal army recovers the land;
Tell your father in the family sacrifice.

译后小记

《示儿》诗为陆游的绝笔，作于宋宁宗嘉定二年十二月（1210年元月）。此时陆游八十五岁，一病不起，在临终前，给儿子们写下了这首诗。这既是诗人的遗嘱，也是诗人发出的最后的抗战号召。

示儿：写给儿子们看。

元知：原本知道。元，通"原"。

但：只是。悲：悲伤。九州：这里代指宋代的中国。古代中国分为九州，所以常用九州指代中国。同：统一。

王师：指南宋朝廷的军队。北定：将北方平定。中原：指淮河以北被金人侵占的地区。

家祭：祭祀家中先人。无忘：不要忘记。乃翁：你的父亲，指陆游自己。

此诗"悲壮沉痛""可泣鬼神"，译文真实地再现了诗人临终时复杂的思想情绪和忧国忧民的爱国情怀。

78. 春日

〔南宋〕朱熹

胜日寻芳泗水滨,
无边光景一时新。
等闲识得东风面,
万紫千红总是春。

78. *Spring Day*

〔the Southern Song Dynasty〕By Zhu Xi

I'm seeking scenes by Si River on a sunny day:
Grass lush, flowers blooming, a thriving way.
Refreshed by a sudden breath of spring in air,
I see in myriads of colors spring hide there.

译后小记

《春日》是宋代思想家、教育家朱熹创作的一首诗。此诗表面上看似一首写景诗,描绘了春日美好的景致;实际上是一首哲理诗,表达了诗人于乱世中追求圣人之道的美好愿望。

胜日:此指晴日。寻芳:游春,踏青。光景:风光,风景。等闲:轻易,寻常,随便。东风面:借指春天。

从字面上看,这首诗好像是写游春观感,但细究寻芳的地点是泗水之滨,而此地在宋南渡时早被金人侵占。朱熹未曾北上,当然不可能在泗水之滨游春吟赏。其实诗中的"泗水"是暗指孔门,因为春秋时孔子曾在洙、泗之间弦歌讲学,教授弟子。因此所谓"寻芳"即是指求圣人之道。"无边光景"所示空间极其广大,就透露了诗人膜求圣道的本意。"东风"暗喻教化,"万紫千红"喻孔学的丰富多彩。诗人将圣人之道比作催发生机、点燃万物的春风。

译者不宜将诗歌的寓意明示,减少读者的审美过程,故"胜日寻芳泗水滨"译为 I'm seeking scenes by Si River on a sunny day;"无边光景一时新",翻译的时候,意象具体化,译为"Grass lush, flowers blooming, a thriving way"。"等闲识得东风面,万紫千红总是春"译为 Refreshed by a sudden breath of spring in air, I see in myriads of colors spring hide there。(春天的气息突然使我精神振奋,我马上意识到春天就藏在万紫千红之中。)

译诗行尾押完全韵 aabb。

79. 观书有感

〔南宋〕朱熹

半亩方塘一鉴开，
天光云影共徘徊。
问渠那得清如许？
为有源头活水来。

79. Reflections on the Book

〔the Southern Song Dynasty〕By Zhu Xi

There lies an oblong pool like a mirror;
In which light and shadows wander.
How could it be so clean and clear?
Because a source brings fresh water.

译后小记

此诗是描绘朱熹"观书"的感受，借助生动的形象揭示深刻的哲理。第一首诗借助池塘水清因有活水注入的现象，比喻要不断接受新事物，才能保持思想的活跃与进步。

此诗英译，每行八至九个音节，主旋律为四音步抑扬格，行尾采用尾元韵，押韵格式为 aaba。虽未押完全韵，但采用英诗"近似韵"（assonance），也能产生平易、自然的声音美。如译诗中，mirror, wander 和 water，押尾元韵。第三行有头韵：could, clean 与 clear 等。

80. 拒霜

〔南宋〕陈与义

拒霜花已吐,
吾宇不凄凉。
天地虽肃杀,
草木有芬芳。
道人宴坐处,
侍女古时妆。
浓露湿丹脸,
西风吹绿裳。

80. *Cotton Rose*

〔the Southern Song Dynasty〕By Chen Yuyi

With cotton roses in full bloom,
No longer is my abode in gloom.
Although it's desperate bleak,
The flora smells fragrant indeed.
In the Taoist meditation place,
The maids are in ancient arrays,
Whose pink faces moist with dew,
Whose dresses in wind a green hue.

译后小记

诗题"拒霜"的英译是个难点，若单纯音译不能表达其义；若按字面直译 the frost-proof blooms，则不知为何种花卉；若用其学名似难出诗意诗境。笔者曾采用音译＋意译，译为 Jushuang, the Frost-Proof Blooms。简洁一点，译为 cotton rose(木芙蓉)也未尝不可，诗文中写的就是拒霜不畏严寒，只是丢失"拒霜"这一中文花名，加大了读者的理解难度。诗无达诂，翻译总是得失之间的选择。

诗歌翻译首先是原诗语篇连贯解读，然后是译诗语篇连贯重构过程。笔者用三种不同的下画线来体现语义的连贯关系，原诗的语义连贯关系，分析如下：

拒霜

拒霜花已吐，吾宇不凄凉。
天地虽肃杀，草木有芬芳。
道人宴坐处，侍女古时妆。
浓露湿丹脸，西风吹绿裳。

译诗语义连贯关系，分析如下：

Cotton Rose

With cotton roses in full bloom,
No longer is my abode in gloom.
Although it's desperate bleak,
The flora smells fragrant indeed.
In the Taoist meditation place,

    The maids are in ancient arrays,
    Whose pink faces moist with dew,
    Whose dresses in wind a green hue.

译诗语篇连贯与原诗一致,行尾押联韵 aabbccdd。

81. 清平乐·村居

〔南宋〕辛弃疾

茅檐低小,
溪上青青草。
醉里吴音相媚好,
白发谁家翁媪?

大儿锄豆溪东,
中儿正织鸡笼。
最喜小儿无赖,
溪头卧剥莲蓬。

81. *Pure Serene Music · Village Life*

〔the Southern Song Dynasty〕By Xin Qiji

The brim of the cottage is small and low;
By a stream green grasses grow.
In soft Wu dialect teasing each other,
Who are the old couple, do you know?

In the bean field, the eldest son is weeding;
A chicken cage, the second son is weaving,
Lying on grass, the naughty little son is peeling
Fresh lotus at the upstream.

译后小记

这首词分上下阕，茅檐、小溪、青草，这本来是农村司空见惯的东西，然而作者把它们组合在一个画面里，却显得格外清新优美。翁媪饮酒聊天，大儿锄草，中儿编鸡笼，小儿卧剥莲蓬。通过这样简单的情节安排，就把一片生机勃勃、和平宁静、朴素安适的农村生活，真实地反映出来了，给人一种诗情画意，清新悦目的感觉。作者对农村景象的描绘，反映了作者的主观情感。

原词音韵和谐，行尾押韵 aaaa bbbb，译词有一定音韵效果，行尾韵为 aaca cccd。

82. 西江月·夜行黄沙道中

〔南宋〕辛弃疾

明月别枝惊鹊,
清风半夜鸣蝉。
稻花香里说丰年,
听取蛙声一片。

七八个星天外,
两三点雨山前。
旧时茅店社林边,
路转溪桥忽见。

82. *The Moon over the West River · A Night Walk on Huangsha Road*

〔the Southern Song Dynasty〕By Xin Qiji

The moon over branch startles a magpie up;
Midnight wind wafts song of cicadas afar.
In rice aroma, a burst of frog comes in ear,
As if chanting the bumper harvest year.

Six or seven stars twinkle in the sky;
A few drops of rain sprinkle by the hillside.

The thatched cottage near the temple in woods,

Across a bridge over a stream, suddenly appears.

译后小记

此词从视觉、听觉、嗅觉三方面描写黄沙岭的夏夜的山村风光。

茅店：茅草盖的乡村客店。社林：土地庙附近的树林。社，土地神庙。古时，村有社树，为祀神处，故曰社林。"社"简单译为 temple。

原词意境优美，音韵和谐，译词只能力求意境，未能押韵。

83. 小池

〔南宋〕杨万里

泉眼无声惜细流,
树阴照水爱晴柔。
小荷才露尖尖角,
早有蜻蜓立上头。

83. *A Small Pond*

〔the Southern Song Dynasty〕By Yang Wanli

So light, so gentle, gurgles a springlet;
A tree cares for it with soft shades.
A little lotus is barely showing its tip;
A dragonfly alights on it next minute.

译后小记

此诗是一首描写初夏池塘美丽景色的、清新的小诗。一切都是那样的细,那样的柔,那样的富有情意,宛如一幅花草虫鸟彩墨画。画面之中,池、泉、流、荷和蜻蜓,落笔都小,却玲珑剔透,生机盎然。

第一句,紧扣题目写小池的源泉,一股涓涓细流的泉水。第二句,写树阴在晴朗柔和的风光里,遮住水面。第三、四句写池中一株小荷以及荷上的蜻蜓。

为表达原诗的"细""柔"之美，译诗诗行中多头韵/s/，如 so 与 springlet，soft 与 shades；一、三、四行尾韵为/ɪ/，译诗避免选用响亮的开元音单词，是不是更好地表达了原诗的轻细柔和之美呢？

译诗是一门有缺陷的艺术，译者只是找到音韵诗意中的一个平衡点。

84. 晓出净慈寺送林子方

〔南宋〕杨万里

毕竟西湖六月中，
风光不与四时同。
接天莲叶无穷碧，
映日荷花别样红。

84. *Seeing off My Friend at Lakeside Temple at Dawn*

〔the Southern Song Dynasty〕By Yang Wanli

West Lake is unique in summer season;
The lotus takes on a charming scene.
Green leaves extent boundless to sky,
Pink flowers in sunlight a thriving sight.

译后小记

这是一首描写西湖六月美丽景色的诗，这首诗是诗中有画，画中有诗的典范作品。通过描写六月西湖的美丽景色，曲折地表达对友人林子方的眷恋之情。

净慈寺：在杭州西湖南岸，全名"净慈报恩光孝禅寺"，与灵隐寺同为杭州西湖南北山两大著名佛寺。英译时，为减轻读者的理解负担，将"净慈寺"译为 Lakeside Temple，简化处理了文化负载信息。

毕竟：到底，言外有名不虚传的意味。翻译时，并不是按字面意思译为 after all，而是用了 unique 来表达西湖独特的美。

四时：春夏秋冬四个季节。在这里指六月以外的其他时节。我国 1949 年正式规定公元纪年，古诗词中的时间，一般都是阴历。诗中的"六月"，译者处理为 summer season。

接天：像与天空相接。无穷碧：因莲叶面积很广，似与天相接，故呈现无边无际的碧绿。别样红：红得特别出色。别样，宋代俗语，特别，不一样。

译诗主旋律为抑扬格四音步，行尾押韵 aabb。

译诗格律分析如下：

West Lake is unique in summer season;
The lotus takes on a charming scene.
Green leaves extent boundless to sky,
Pink flowers in sunlight a thriving sight.

85. 宿新市徐公店

〔南宋〕杨万里

篱落疏疏一径深,
树头花落未成阴。
儿童急走追黄蝶,
飞入菜花无处寻。

85. *An Overnight Stay at the Xu's Inn*

〔the Southern Song Dynasty〕By Yang Wanli

Hedge sparse, a lane leads to a deep side;
Petals fallen, trees are not yet crowned.
A yellow butterfly, chased by a kid around,
Flutters into yellow flowers of rape to hide.

译后小记

这是一首描写暮春农村景色的诗歌,选取篱落、菜花、儿童、黄蝶等意象,描绘了一幅春意盎然的景象。

新市:地名。今浙江省德清县新市镇,一说在今湖北省京山县东北。徐公店:姓徐的人家开的酒店名。英译时,地名略去不译。

头二句"篱落疏疏一径深,树头花落未成阴"(一作"树头新绿未成阴"),点出时间大概是春末。画面上有一道稀疏的篱笆和一条幽深的小路，篱笆旁还有棵树，花瓣纷纷飘落，新叶刚刚长出还尚未形成树荫，树叶如同树冠。故译为结构对称的两行 Hedge sparse, a lane leads to a deep side; Petals fallen, trees are not yet crowned。也可译为 By hedge sparse, a lane leads to a far side; Leaves just sprout, trees are yet to be crowned。

末二句"儿童急走追黄蝶，飞入菜花无处寻"将彩笔转入画面的中心，描绘儿童捕蝶的欢乐场面。译诗采用拟人手法，用了 hide 表示蝴蝶飞入菜花藏起来的情景，富有童趣。

译诗流畅自然，行尾押抱韵 abba。

86. 夏夜追凉

〔南宋〕杨万里

夜热依然午热同,
开门小立月明中。
竹深树密虫鸣处,
时有微凉不是风。

86. *Seeking Cool on Summer Night*

〔the Southern Song Dynasty〕By Yang Wanli

It's hot the same at night as at noon;
I open the door and stand in the moon.
Crickets chirp from bamboos and trees;
The air is cool but not for the breeze.

译后小记

"追凉",即觅凉、取凉。较之"觅"和"取","追"更能表现对"凉"的渴求。诗人撇开了暑热难耐的感受,而仅就"追凉"着墨,以淡淡的几笔,勾勒出一幅夏夜追凉图,其中有皎洁的月光,有浓密的树荫,有婆娑的竹林,有悦耳的虫吟,以及作者悄然伫立的身影。

第三句是对周围环境的点染:竹林深深,树荫密密,虫鸣唧唧。"竹深树密",见其清幽;"虫鸣",则见其静谧——唯其静谧,"虫鸣"

之声才能清晰入耳。诗人置身其间，凉意顿生，于是又引出结句"时有微凉不是风"，这一真切、细微的体验——静中生凉正是作者所要表现的意趣。

译诗主旋律为抑扬格四音步，行尾押完全韵 aabb。

译诗格律分析如下：

It's <u>hot</u> the <u>same</u> at <u>night</u> as at <u>noon</u>;
I <u>open</u> the <u>door</u> and <u>stand</u> in the <u>moon</u>.
Crickets <u>chirp</u> from bam<u>boos</u> and <u>trees</u>;
The <u>air</u> is <u>cool</u> but <u>not</u> for the <u>breeze</u>.

87. 舟过安仁

〔南宋〕杨万里

一叶渔船两小童,
收篙停棹坐船中。
怪生无雨都张伞,
不是遮头是使风。

87. *Going by Anren on Boat*

〔the Southern Song Dynasty〕By Yang Wanli

Two children sit on a fishing boat;
Done with the oars, done with the pole.
They open umbrellas not for rain
To shield, but sailing wind to gain.

译后小记

这首七言绝句,浅白如话,充满情趣,展示了无忧无虑的两个小渔童的充满童稚的行为,其行为中透出了只有儿童才有的奇思妙想与聪慧,体现了两小童的可爱与思维的敏捷。

安仁:县名,1914年因与湖南安仁县同名而改名余江县。英译时,地名音译。

译诗主旋律为抑扬格四音步,行尾押韵 aabb。

译诗格律分析如下：

Two children sit on a fishing boat;
Done with the oars, done with the pole.
They open umbrellas not for rain
To shield, but sailing wind to gain.

88. 乡村四月

〔南宋〕翁卷

绿遍山原白满川，
子规声里雨如烟。
乡村四月闲人少，
才了蚕桑又插田。

88. *Late Spring in the Countryside*

〔The Southern Song Dynasty〕By Weng Juan

The hills are green, the paddy fields white;
In cuckoos' singing the misty drizzles fine.
In April the countryside is in prime time;
Sericulture is followed by planting rice.

译后小记

此诗以清新明快的笔调，出神入化地描写了江南农村初夏时节的旖旎风光，表达了诗人对乡村生活的热爱之情。

前两句写自然景象。"绿"，写树木葱郁，"白"，写水光映天。举目望去，绿油油的禾田，白茫茫的水，全都笼罩在那如烟似雾的蒙蒙细雨中，不时有几声布谷鸟的呼唤从树上、空中传来。首句"绿遍山原白满川"的英译（The hills are green, the paddy fields white）省略了谓语动词 are。

次句"子规声里雨如烟"(In cuckoos' singing the misty drizzles fine),如烟似雾的细雨好像是被子规的鸣叫唤来的,此句译文语法结构可有不同解释,drizzle 可作名词,也可作动词,fine,有"好的""细小的"等义项,希望能产生出原诗意境。

后两句"乡村四月闲人少,才了蚕桑又插田"(In April the countryside is in prime time;／Sericulture is followed by planting rice)歌咏江南初夏的繁忙农事,原诗不正面直说人们太忙,译诗结合谚语"一年之计在于春",联想到 prime time,也契合原诗诗意。

译诗有一定音韵节奏,主旋律为抑扬格五音步,行尾押元韵 aaaa。

89. 丙申元旦守母制因感而作

〔元〕王冕

今日椒花颂,
无能献老亲。
自怜垂白发,
不敢着乌巾。
牢落田园兴,
微茫海国春。
话言儿女辈,
清苦莫辞贫。

89. Sentiments on the Lunar New Year in Observing Mourning for My Mother

〔Yuan Dynasty〕By Wang Mian

A New Year greeting to whom?
My old parents are laid in tomb.
A stab of pity for my grey hair,
A black scarf-hat, I fear to wear.
The countryside is full of power;
Spring will see a sea of flower.
May you remember, my dears,
Lead a simple life, shed no tears.

译后小记

丙申年是 1356 年，这一年王冕 70 岁，因母亲去世，王冕正在守孝。

诗中的"元旦"，指旧历新年。

守制：指守孝，遵行居丧的制度。旧时，父母或祖父母去世后，儿子或长孙需在家守孝 27 个月，在此期间不得婚嫁、应考、上任，现任官员需离任。

椒花颂：典故名，指新年祝词。典出《晋书》卷九十六《列女传·刘臻妻陈氏传》。晋人刘臻的妻子陈氏，聪慧能写文章，曾经在正月初一献《椒花颂》。后遂用为典实，指新年祝词，这里译为 a New Year greeting。

乌巾：即乌角巾，古代多为隐居不仕者的帽子，这里译为 a black scarf-hat。

牢落：稀疏零落貌、零落荒芜貌。

此诗中的文化负载词是翻译的难点，英译时，有些文化负载信息省略。原诗是五言律诗，"亲""巾""贫"押韵工整。译诗押韵，格式为 aabbccdd。

90. 天净沙·秋

〔元〕白朴

孤村落日残霞,
轻烟老树寒鸦,
一点飞鸿影下。
青山绿水,
白草红叶黄花。

90. *Clear Sand · Autumn*

〔Yuan Dynasty〕By Bai Pu

A lone village sees the setting sun glow,
Wisps of smoke, an old tree, a raven crow;
A wild goose's shadow throws.
The hills are green, the rills blue,
Grasses white, leaves red, flowers yellow.

译后小记

《天净沙·秋》是元代曲作家白朴创作的一首写景散曲,作者通过撷取十二种景物,描绘出一幅景色从萧瑟、寂寥到明朗、清丽的秋景图。

前二句的"孤村落日残霞,轻烟老树寒鸦",共用了六个意象:"孤村""落日""残霞""轻烟""老树""寒鸦",而其中任何一个意象,都代表着秋日秋景的萧瑟气氛。为了使这种萧瑟气氛活泼起来,于是作者接下来选用了"一点飞鸿影下"作为上半段的结语。如此一来,原本萧瑟的画面转成了活跃、寂寞的秋景,仿佛也展现了另一种鲜活的生气。最后为了加强作者心目中秋景是美丽而有韵味的形象,因此再以"青山绿水,白草红叶黄花"作为曲文的结束语。这两句用了"青""绿""白""红""黄"五种颜色,而且"白草红叶黄花"这三种颜色,是交杂在"青山绿水"两种颜色之中;"青山绿水"是广大的图景,"白草红叶黄花"是细微的图景,如此交杂相错,于是原本寂寞萧瑟的秋景,突然变得五颜六色而多姿多彩起来。

翻译时尽量再现原曲的意象和图景,有一定音韵节奏,行尾押韵格式同原曲 aaaba。

91. 画鸡

〔明〕唐寅

头上红冠不用裁，
满身雪白走将来。
平生不敢轻言语，
一叫千门万户开。

91. *A Painting of a Rooster*

〔Ming Dynasty〕By Tang Yin

On head a natural scarlet crown,
It strides ahead in a snowy gown.
As usual it keeps its voice so low,
Because the doors will ope at its crow.

译后小记

《画鸡》是明代诗人唐寅为自己的画作题写的一首七言绝句。这首诗描绘了雄鸡的威武和高洁，把鸡的神态气质和报晓天性展现得淋漓尽致。

"头上红冠不用裁，满身雪白走将来"，这是写雄鸡的动作、神态。诗人运用了描写和色彩的对比，勾画了一只冠红羽白、威风凛凛、相貌堂堂的大公鸡，头戴无须剪裁的天然红冠，一身雪白，兴致冲冲地迎面走来。这里的"走"，笔者译为 stride，而不用 tiptoe，以免产生怯生生之感。

"平生不敢轻言语，一叫千门万户开。"这是写雄鸡的心理和声音。这里的"不敢"，笔者认为不应理解为公鸡胆小，而是公鸡的低调，一生不轻易随便啼叫，因为它一声鸣叫，千家万户都要打开门，迎接新的一天的到来。故笔者不用 dare not 之类的表达，而译为"As usual it keeps its voice so low"（雄鸡像往常一样不言语），然后"because"一词道出原因，将三四句联系起来，这样前后语义连贯一致。

翻译此诗，译者特别注意画面的流畅，前后语义连贯，雄鸡的威武形象前后一致。译诗为抑扬格四音步，行尾押联韵 aabb。原诗格律分析如下：

On head a natural scarlet crown,
It strides ahead in a snowy gown.
As usual it keeps its voice so low,
Because the doors will ope at its crow.

92. 次韵陆佥宪元日春晴

〔明〕王守仁

城里夕阳城外雪,
相将十里异阴晴。
也知造物曾何意,
底事人心苦未平。
柏府楼台衔倒影,
茅茨松竹泻寒声。
布衾莫谩愁僵卧,
积素还多达曙明。

92. Spring Clear, Written According to the Rhyming Words of New Year's Day by Lu Qianxian

〔Ming Dynasty〕By Wang Shouren

It's sunny in town, but snowy outside;
So different between ten miles wide!
But who can read the Creator's mind,
Could it be the suffering he doesn't find?
The palace reflected in water is dazzling,
The hut in bamboos and pines freezing.

Add a quilt, worry not about a cold night;
The snow is still deep before the twilight.

译后小记

这首诗写初春的景象，诗中看似写"相将十里异阴晴"的气候现象，实则表达诗人关心老百姓的疾苦。城里"夕阳"城外"雪"，难道是造物主忘记了受苦的大众吗？城里"柏府楼台"，城外"茅茨松竹"，亦是富人和穷人住所的对比；最后是希望穷人等到天明，保持对美好未来的强烈愿望。

次韵：旧时古体诗词写作的一种方式。按照原诗的韵和用韵的次序来和诗。

也知：有谁知道。

底：作疑问代词，相当于"何"。

柏府：御史府的别称，泛指豪宅。

茅茨：茅屋。

布衾：布被，如杜甫诗《茅屋为秋风所破歌》："布衾多年冷似铁。"诗中转喻，类似"布衣"指代老百姓，这里指"茅茨"中人，英译时，祈使句省略主语。

谩愁：担心。

积素：积雪。

此诗翻译的重点在于理解诗中"意象"所指，原诗为七律，拙译取联韵 aabbccdd。

93. 临江仙

〔明〕杨慎

滚滚长江东逝水，
浪花淘尽英雄。
是非成败转头空。
青山依旧在，
几度夕阳红。

白发渔樵江渚上，
惯看秋月春风。
一壶浊酒喜相逢。
古今多少事，
都付笑谈中。

93. Riverside Daffodils

〔Ming Dynasty〕By Yang Shen

Eastward the Yangtze River flows;
Sprays disappear with the heroes.
Right or wrong, success or failure, let it go.
The hills are still green so,
Seeing the sun rise and glow.

A gray-haired hermit by the riverside

Is accustomed to changes of times.

Sharing a pot of wine, they are delight.

Things through ages fly by

When they talk jolly and high.

译后小记

1511年(明朝正德六年)，杨慎获殿试第一。1524年因得罪明世宗朱厚熜，杨慎被发配到云南充军。他戴着枷锁，被军士押解到湖北江陵时，正好一个渔夫和一个柴夫在江边煮鱼喝酒，谈笑风生。杨慎突然很感慨，于是请军士找来纸笔，写下《临江仙》。

诗歌语言简洁凝练，译诗也尽量语言简洁。上片押尾韵/əʊ/，下片押尾韵/aɪ/。

94. 长相思

〔清〕纳兰性德

山一程,
水一程,
身向榆关那畔行,
夜深千帐灯。

风一更,
雪一更,
聒碎乡心梦不成,
故园无此声。

94. *Everlasting Yearning*

〔Qing Dynasty〕By Nalan Xingde

We climb up the hills;
We then cross the rills.
Towards Pass Yuguan, we move on and on.
Late at night the tents are alight.

The cold wind lashes;
Heauy snow slashes;
The snowstorm makes hearts broken and sleepless.
No such a sound at homeland.

译后小记

译诗戴着镣铐跳舞,尝试赵彦春教授的古诗词翻译原则:三言类比为五音节、四言类比为六音节、五言类比为八音节、六言类比为九音节、七言类比为十音节、八言类比为十二音节、九言类比为十四音节。

原词上下阕字数分别为:3,3,7,5。译文上下两部分音节数分别为5,5,10,8;语义与原词一致,节奏相当。"千帐灯"的"千"是虚数,英译时省略不译。

95. 村居

〔清〕高鼎

草长莺飞二月天,
拂堤杨柳醉春烟。
儿童散学归来早,
忙趁东风放纸鸢。

95. *A Village Scene*

〔Qing Dynasty〕By Gao Ding

Midspring sees grasses grow and orioles fly;
Willows dance in mist fondling the bank slight.
The children, returning home early from school,
Hurriedly in the east wind fly the paper kite.

译后小记

此诗是诗人晚年归隐于上饶地区、闲居农村时创作的一首七言绝句。

第一、第二句写时间和自然景物,具体生动地描写了春天里的大自然,写出了春日农村特有的明媚、迷人的景色;"二月"是农历二月,不是公历 February,据典籍"二月仲春",可译为 midspring;"草长""莺飞""拂堤杨柳""春烟"几个意象,在译诗中再现。

第三、第四句写的是人物活动,描述了一群活泼的儿童在大好的春光里放风筝的生动情景。"儿童散学归来早,忙趁东风放纸鸢",可调整为"散学归来早(的)儿童忙趁东风放纸鸢",译诗三四行为跨行诗句,用了一个插入语 returning home early from school,主句为 The children…hurriedly in the east wind fly the paper kite。

译诗行尾押不完全韵,格式为 aaba。

96. 绮怀诗

〔清〕黄景仁

几回花下坐吹箫,
银汉红墙入望遥。
似此星辰非昨夜,
为谁风露立中宵。
缠绵思尽抽残茧,
宛转心伤剥后蕉。
三五年时三五月,
可怜杯酒不曾消。

96. *Love Is but a Dream*

〔Qing Dynasty〕By Huang Jingren

We used to play flute under the flowering tree;
Now the red wall is the Milky Way far from me.
The stars are no longer bright as yester night.
For whom I stand in wind and dew till midnight?
Dying of lovesick I'm a cocoon drawn out of silk
With a broken heart delicate as a banana peeled.
Gone are the glorious months in those years.
The bitterness in the wine never disappears.

译后小记

"绮怀"是一种美丽的情怀,对清代诗人黄景仁来说,这种美丽来自一种爱情失落无处寻觅的绝望,因而更加凄婉动人。故译诗题为 Love is but a dream。

首联"几回花下坐吹箫,银汉红墙入望遥。"(We used to play flute under the flowering tree; Now the red wall is the Milky Way far from me)明月相伴,花下吹箫,美好的相遇。但是这只是一个开始。那伊人所在的红墙虽然近在咫尺,却如天上的银河一般遥不可及。故翻译时加上 far from me,突出这种遥不可及的心理感受。

第二联"似此星辰非昨夜,为谁风露立中宵。"(The stars are no longer bright as yester night. For whom I stand in wind and dew till midnight?)今夜已非昨夜,昨夜的星辰,是记录着花下吹箫的浪漫故事,而今夜的星辰,却只有陪伴自己这个伤心之人,往事不可能重现,诗人陷入了更深的绝望。

第三联"缠绵思尽抽残茧,宛转心伤剥后蕉。"(Dying of lovesick I'm a cocoon drawn out of silk/ With a broken heart delicate as a banana peeled.)春蚕吐丝,将自己重重包裹,正如诗人自己,用重重思念将自己重重包围。

尾联"三五年时三五月"自然是"几回花下坐吹箫"的往昔,译诗没有照字面来译,而是转换为"那些年的好时光一去不复返了"(Gone are the glorious months in those years)。

97. 对月寓怀

〔清〕曹雪芹

时逢三五便团圆,
满把晴光护玉栏。
天上一轮才捧出,
人间万姓仰头看。

97. A Lyric to the Full Moon

〔Qing Dynasty〕By Cao Xueqing

The moon is full bright on the fifteenth night;
The jade handrails are enveloped in the light.
The moment the moon shows up in the sky,
All people are prompt to look up at her sight.

译后小记

首句的"三五"指农历每月十五,"时逢三五便团圆"便译为 The moon is full bright on the fifteenth night;"满把晴光护玉栏",译诗采用认知转换视角,译为 The jade handrails are enveloped in the light(玉栏杆被月色笼罩)。

后两句"天上一轮才捧出,人间万姓仰头看。"(The moment the moon shows up in the sky, all people are prompt to look up at her sight.)

隐喻贾雨村一旦"时逢"机会就爬上令人仰望敬畏的高位,老百姓唯有仰视之。

译诗行尾押完全韵 aaba,与原诗相同。

98. 山中雪后

〔清〕郑燮

晨起开门雪满山,
雪晴云淡日光寒。
檐流未滴梅花冻,
一种清孤不等闲。

98. The Hill-Scene After Snow

〔Qing Dynasty〕By Zheng Xie

Opening a door in morn, I see hills a world silver;
Snow thick, cloud thin, hazy daylight seems shiver.
Eave icicles yet to drip, plum blooms frozen sheer,
All are glittering lonely light, graceful, lofty and clear.

译后小记

这是一首白描诗,也是一幅雪景山水画。前两句写清晨雪后,大地银装素裹,旭日东升,天气寒冷的景象。

"晨起开门雪满山"(Opening a door in morn, I see hills a world silver),"雪满山"在译文里转化为"银装素裹的世界";"雪晴云淡日光寒"(Snow thick, cloud thin, hazy daylight seems shiver),译文转化为"厚厚的积雪、淡淡的云、朦胧的日光透着寒意,似乎打着寒颤"。

后两句通过"檐流未滴"突出了天气的寒冷,"清孤不等闲"突出了梅花清高坚韧的性格和洁身自好的品质。"檐流(溜)"指屋檐下的冰柱子,英译为 eave icicles。

原诗是七绝,译文采用对句联韵 aabb,且有行内头韵。

99. 惠州西湖玩月

〔清〕吴骞

茫茫水月漾湖天，
人在苏堤千顷边。
多少管窥夸见月，
可知月在此间圆？

99. Admiring the Moon by Lake

〔Qing Dynasty〕By Wu Qian

The water joins the moonlit sky at the horizon;
The tourists meander along the vast Su Dyke.
Those who boasts seeing the moon in the sky,
Do you know the moon is full just in this time?

译后小记

"苏堤玩月"，是广东省惠州西湖的一个名胜景点。北宋苏轼贬谪惠州时带头筑造了"苏堤"，后人建"苏公桥"纪念之。农历每月十五月圆之夜，人们在此赏玩月下湖景，充满诗情画意。此诗写的就是"苏堤玩月"。

前两句写月下西湖广阔无边，充满诗情画意；后两句写西湖赏月，恰逢月圆。

译诗在理解原诗基础上来表达，行尾押不完全韵 aaaa。

100. 《儒林外史》中的一首宝塔诗

呆

秀　才

吃　长　斋

胡　须　满　腮

经　书　揭　不　开

纸　笔　自　己　安　排

明　年　不　请　我　自　来

100. A shape poem *in The Scholars*

Poor

Bookish scholar

Fasted long period

Cheeks with unkempt whiskers

For classics he's a non-reader

Brushes and paper, he'd always prepare

He'd come without being invited next year

译后小记

一字至七字诗，俗称宝塔诗，在中国古代诗中较为少见。此诗以宝塔形状构建全诗，匠心独特，可谓"形美感目"。全诗 7 行，字数逐行增加，形成诗歌独特的形貌。原诗行尾押韵，可谓"音美感耳"。此诗讽刺迂腐秀才，年纪一大把，不求上进，以教书混饭吃，非常深刻，可谓"意美感人"。

译诗7行，每行单词数为1，2，3，4，5，6，7，单词数的逐行变化，再现宝塔形诗。译诗紧贴原诗，传承原诗诗意，"意美"不逊原诗。译诗行尾不押韵，但有一定音韵效果，有/ə/音回响。

翻译难得完美，译者就是在"音美""形美""意美"之间，寻求一个最佳平衡点。

参 考 文 献

[1] Beaugrande R de, Dressler W. Introduction to text linguistics[M]. London & New York: Longman, 1981: 3-13.

[2] Catford J C. A linguistic theory of translation [M]. Oxford: Oxford University Press, 1965.

[3] Christiane Nord. Translating as a purposeful activity-functionalist approaches explained [M]. Shanghai: Shanghai Foreign Language Education Press, 2001.

[4] Fussel Paul. Poetic meter and poetic form[M]. New York: Random House, 1965.

[5] Jakobson R. What is poetry? [M] // Jakobson R. Language in literature. Massachusetts and London: The Belknap Press of Harvard University Press, 1987: 368-378.

[6] Halliday M A K, Hasan R. Cohesion in English [M]. Shanghai: Foreign Language and Research Press, 2001.

[7] McAuley J. *Versification*: A short introduction[M]. East Lansing: Michigan State University Press, 1966.

[8] Papegaaij B, Schubert K. Text coherence in translation [M]. Dordrecht: Foris Publication, 1988.

[9] Shklovsky V. Art as technique[C]//David Lodge. Modern criticism and theory: a reader. London: Longman, 1988: 20.

[10] Todorov T. The poetics of prose[M]. Ithaca, New York: Cornell University, 1977.

[11] Todorov T. Introduction to poetics[M]. Minneapolis: University of

Minnesota Press, 1981.

[12] 卞之琳. 英国诗选[M]. 北京：商务印书馆, 1996.

[13] 陈刚. 西湖诗赞[M]. 杭州：浙江摄影出版社, 1996.

[14] 陈宏薇. 汉英翻译基础[M]. 上海：上海外语教育出版社, 1998.

[15] 陈君朴. 汉英对照唐诗绝句150首[M]. 上海：上海大学出版社, 2005.

[16] 丰华瞻. 丰华瞻译诗集[M]. 上海：上海外语教育出版社, 1997.

[17] 冯庆华. 红译艺坛[M]. 上海：上海外语教育出版社, 2006.

[18] 搞口译的也可以留芳[EB/OL]. [2007-05-02]. http://www.tianya.cn/publicforum/content/english/1/117292.shtml.

[19] Milkias Mehreteab Yohannes. It is better to die *a thousand times than live without dignity*[EB/OL]. [2011-01-23]. http://awate.com/category/articles.

[20] 辜正坤, 译注. 毛泽东诗词：英汉对照韵译[M]. 北京：北京大学出版社, 1993.

[21] 顾正阳. 古诗词曲英译美学研究[M]. 上海：上海大学出版社, 2006.

[22] 郭建中. 当代美国翻译理论[M]. 武汉：湖北教育出版社, 2000.

[23] 黄杲炘. 英诗汉译学[M]. 上海：上海外语教育出版社, 2007.

[24] 黄杲炘, 译. 柔巴依一百首[M]. 北京：中国对外翻译出版公司, 1998.

[25] 江枫. 论文学翻译及汉语汉字[M]. 北京：华文出版社, 2009.

[26] 李云启. 英诗赏读与美感再植[M]. 北京：人民出版社, 2007.

[27] 刘坤尊. 英诗的音韵格律[M]. 桂林：广西师范大学出版社, 2011.

[28] 罗良功. 英诗概论[M]. 武汉：武汉大学出版社, 2002.

[29] 罗义蕴, 曹明伦, 陈朴. 英诗金库[M]. 成都：四川人民出版社,

[30] 毛荣贵. 新世纪大学英汉翻译教程[M]. 上海：上海交通大学出版社，2002.

[31] 毛泽东. 纪念白求恩[M]. 北京：东方红出版社，1967.

[32] 穆诗雄. 诗歌鉴赏的差异性与诗歌翻译[J]. 外语与外语教学，2005(2)：33-36.

[33] 聂珍钊. 英语诗歌形式导论[M]. 北京：中国社会科学出版社，2007.

[34] 潘文国. "语文歧视"会引发汉语危机吗[N]. 解放日报，2011-2-7(5).

[35] 蒲度戎. 押韵诗歌欣赏[M]. 重庆：重庆大学出版社，2008.

[36] 齐晓燕. 英诗的美学探究[M]. 北京：中国传媒大学出版社，2008.

[37] 沈苏儒. 翻译的最高境界"信达雅"漫谈[M]. 北京：中国对外翻译出版公司，2006.

[38] 施仲谋，等. 中华文化承传(上册)[M]. 北京：北京大学出版社，2007.

[39] 石璞. 英诗初阶[M]. 西安：西北工业大学出版社，1987.

[40] 宋天锡. 翻译新概念：英汉互译实用教程[M]. 北京：国防工业出版社，2007.

[41] 唐一鹤，注译. 英译唐诗三百首[M]. 天津：天津人民出版社，2005.

[42] 涂宗涛. 诗词曲格律纲要[M]. 天津：天津人民出版社，2000.

[43] 《毛泽东诗词》翻译组. 毛泽东诗词[M]. 北京：外文出版社，1999.

[44] 汪榕培. 英译陶诗[M]. 北京：商务印书馆，1996.

[45] 王大濂. 英译唐诗绝句百首[M]. 天津：百花文艺出版社，1997.

[46] 王东风. 诗意与诗意的翻译[J]. 外语研究, 2018(1): 56-64.

[47] 王东风. 小说翻译的语义连贯重构[J]. 中国翻译, 2005(3): 37-43.

[48] 王东风. 连贯与翻译[M]. 上海: 上海外语教育出版社, 2009.

[49] 王雪松. 论标点符号与中国现代诗歌节奏的关系[J]. 中国现代文学研究丛刊, 2016(3): 158-174.

[50] 王永泰. 旅游广告及俗语外译的艺术美[J]. 上海翻译, 2007(1).

[51] 吴伟雄, 吴庆雯. 新编英汉翻译速通[M]. 武汉: 武汉大学出版社, 2009.

[52] 吴伟雄. 好易学英汉笔译[M]. 广州: 世界图书出版公司, 2000.

[53] 吴伟雄. 谈涉外活动中诗词佳句汉英翻译的现场效果[J]. 上海科技翻译, 2004(1): 28-31.

[54] 吴翔林. 英语格律诗及自由诗[M]. 北京: 商务印书馆, 1993.

[55] 谢天振. 当代国外翻译理论导读[M]. 天津: 南开大学出版社, 2008.

[56] 许渊冲. 翻译的标准[J]. 翻译通讯, 1981(1): 1.

[57] 许渊冲. 翻译的艺术[M]. 北京: 五洲传播出版社, 2006.

[58] 许渊冲. 汉英对照唐诗三百首[M]. 北京: 高等教育出版社, 2000.

[59] 许渊冲. 文学与翻译[M]. 北京: 北京大学出版社, 2003.

[60] 许渊冲. 英汉对照唐诗三百首[M]. 北京: 高等教育出版社, 2001.

[61] 许渊冲. 中诗英韵探胜[M]. 北京: 北京大学出版社, 1992.

[62] 许渊冲. 山阴道上[M]. 北京: 中央编译出版社, 2005.

[63] 许渊冲. 诗书人生[M]. 天津: 百花文艺出版社, 2003: 96.

[64] 许渊冲. 文学与翻译[M]. 北京: 北京大学出版社, 2003.

[65] 许渊冲,等. 唐诗三百首新译[M]. 北京:中国对外翻译出版公司,1998.

[66] 许渊冲,译. 楚辞[M]. 长沙:湖南出版社,1994.

[67] 许渊冲,译. 毛泽东诗词选[M]. 北京:中国对外翻译出版公司,1993.

[68] 许渊冲. 汉英对照宋词三百首[M]. 北京:高等教育出版社,2004.

[69] 许渊冲. 唐诗三百首:汉英对照(2版). 北京:五洲传播出版社,2018.

[70] 杨宪益,戴乃迭. 楚辞选[M]. 北京:外文出版社,2001.

[71] 臧克家. 毛泽东诗词鉴赏[M]. 郑州:河南文艺出版社,2005.

[72] 张美芳. 翻译研究的功能途径[M]. 上海:上海外语教育出版社,2005.

[73] 张智中. 汉诗英译的标点之美[J]. 井冈山大学学报(社会科学版),2015(2):100-105.

[74] 张智中. 汉诗英译美学研究[M]. 北京:商务印书馆,2015.

[75] 郑鉴枢. 楹联讲座[M]. 深圳:海天出版社,1993.

[76] 周领顺. 英译汉之"好":好在哪里?[J]. 西安外国语大学学报,2018(4).

[77] 周领顺. 从文化解读到语言定位[J]. 中国翻译,2018(6):108-111.

[78] 周仪,罗平. 翻译与批评[M]. 武汉:湖北教育出版社,1999.

[79] 追求"信、达、雅"杨宪益获翻译文化终身成就奖[EB/OL]. [2009-09-17]. http://www.china.com.cn/culture/txt/2009-09/17/content_18547077.htm.